Tyto
The Odyssey of an Owl

Illustrated by Dick Kramer

Lothrop, Lee & Shepard Company
A Division of William Morrow & Company, Inc.
NEW YORK

Tyto

The Odyssey of an Owl

by Glyn Frewer

1   2   3   4   5   6   7   8   9   10

Library of Congress Cataloging in Publication Data
Frewer, Glyn.   Tyto: the odyssey of an owl.
SUMMARY: A barn owl completes the hazardous journey
to adulthood and independence.
1. Barn owl—Legends and stories.   [1. Owls—Fiction]
I. Kramer, Dick.   II. Title.
PZ10.3.F888Ty   [Fic]   77-2769
ISBN 0-688-41814-7   ISBN 0-688-51814-1 lib. bdg.

to all who live at Eden End

Contents

Barn Owl *(Tyto alba)*

Class: Aves
Order: Strigiformes
Family: Tytonidae
Genus: *Tyto*

also known as Screech Owl, Church Owl, White Owl,
Yellow Owl, Hissing Owl, Howlet, Gillihowter, Cail-
leach-oidhche-gheal (White night-hag)

1

First Flight

It was the year of the drought, the driest June since 1877. The reservoir levels fell, the riverbanks steepened, many streams disappeared altogether. Merford was lucky. On the village green was a spring which seemingly came from the bowels of the earth: for however long a heat wave lasted and however the rest of the country fared, Merford Pond never ran dry.

The green, some four acres of sheep-nibbled, goat-grazed common land punctuated by hawthorns, became an oasis. The pond's permanent residents, the mallards, coots and moorhens, now shared it not only with the regular visitors, the sparrows and starlings from the tousled thatches of the cottages lining the green, and the jackdaws, swifts, swallows and martins, but with birds from much further afield: skylarks, lapwings and partridges from the parched downlands, jays, woodpeckers and chiffchaffs from the heat-hazed woods. And when Colonel Pickstock (Retired) crossed the green on his midday migration to the Harrow Pub, he saw an owl on the fallen willow, sipping the green water.

The Colonel reported the sighting to Jack the barman.

"First time I've ever seen that, Jack. Big white face, he had, like a little old man. He wouldn't have come down like that unless he was practically dying of thirst."

"Ay, that'll be the old barney from Sam Holdern's farm, I reckon. Always a pair nestin' there, regular every year. Sam likes 'em there, 'e does. 'E says a barn owl keeps 'is rats down better'n that official rat catcher they sent. All *he* done was p'ison the cat!"

"Well, I have heard a barn owl can catch ten rats a night," said the Colonel. "That makes them the farmer's friend all right, and everyone else's I should think."

Jack shook his head. "Dunno about that, Colonel. There's plenty in Merford that'd shoot any owl on sight. Old Jed Coulter for one, 'im as looks after the Park pheasants. 'E'd kill anything as wasn't a pheasant, if you ask me, but 'e's dead set against owls and 'awks and the like. An' Merford folk themselves, they'd shoot an owl. 'Arbingers o' doom, they call 'em, an' I'm not sayin' they're wrong."

"That's rubbish, Jack, that is. Old wives' tales. I've seen dozens of owls and they've never had any ring of doom about them, ever!"

Jack leaned on the bar and stabbed the air with his finger. "Then what about the one you just seen, then?

You said yourself, you only saw 'im out there 'cos things is so bad with the drought."

The Colonel stared at Jack and made no reply.

When the Colonel had stopped at the pond's edge, Barney, who had been watching his approach for five minutes, carried on drinking. Forty feet of water separated them and the owl felt in no danger. Sure enough, the man walked on, leaving him to satisfy his thirst in peace. Nevertheless, settling to a drink in broad daylight in an area filled with humans was not something Barney was used to. On the contrary, he had never done such a thing until today. But he'd been driven to it. The heat of the sun in the southwest corner of the barn where he was roosting had forced him out. Back there, sitting on four white, round eggs, his mate Strega crouched with beak agape, riveted there by the tapping in the egg that had begun that morning.

Barney tossed some moisture from his beak onto the downy feathers of his breast. Every drop that he could carry back would be appreciated by Strega, who would preen his feathers, relishing the moisture.

Enough time here! With slow wing flaps, Barney lifted himself from the willow without making a sound. Across the shimmering heat of the green, he winged his way towards the farm a mile distant. The bright sun hurt his eyes. He felt uneasy, out of his element. He swooped to the shade of the poplars near the road. Five minutes there restored his confidence and he was off again towards the red slate roofs.

Ten minutes later he came in through the door of the loft and landed on the crossbeam. A low mewing from the ledge below the roof greeted him, and another sound, a tuneless note, feeble and plaintive but full of the music of life. Uttering what sounded suspiciously like a chuckle, Barney flew to the nest. Strega tapped at his beak with her own. He opened his beak and she took the minute drops of water which were left. Then she preened the length of his feathers and the moisture eased her thirst a little. From under her wing, the male chick from the first egg of the clutch wriggled blindly. Barney looked down at the hairless, wrinkled shape with its bulbous blind eyes and grotesque egg-tooth beak and grunted. It was his first glimpse of Tyto, the owl born in the heat of the sun, and he was well pleased.

For four days, Tyto was the only chick in the nest. Strega, true to her kind, did not lay eggs like other birds, the whole clutch in one or perhaps two days, but spaced them over several-day intervals. The previous year, her sixth egg had hatched out alongside a four-week-old chick. This spacing was an insurance against a dearth of food. Better one or two survivors than four starving all at once. For four days, Tyto was the sole recipient of the shrews and insects and mice that both parents brought him. By the time Pila, his sister chick, had hatched, Tyto had already trebled his birth weight. Two days passed before Hessa, the second female chick, broke out, and Bur, the second male chick, hatched two days later. This meant that Tyto's growth rate continued faster than the others because, being larger, he was able to grab what food he needed. When he was satisfied, the next in size took the food, until finally all were fed. In Strega's previous brood, the sixth chick to hatch was always outgrabbed and lived only three days.

Feeding four gaping beaks was a full-time occupation for the parent birds. They made their hunting forays not only at night, though that was when they were most successful, but also during the day. Below the nest, the regurgitated pellets of shrews and beetles, cockchafers and moths accumulated at the rate of eight to ten a day.

Ten days after Tyto's birth, Barney flew in at dawn with a mouse. This time, however, instead of tearing the corpse into shreds to feed to the chicks, the big owl pinned the mouse to the beam with his claw and tore off the head, which he swallowed himself. The remainder he passed to the clamoring Tyto, who swallowed the headless carcass in one gulp. Beside him the other chicks hissed for their share, which Strega brought a few minutes later in the form of a frog.

Tyto grew rapidly. His plaintive mews and hisses gave way now to a sibilant snore, a sound which, at dusk, came eerily out to the ears of Sam Holdern and his son as they walked across the yard.

The fourteen-year-old boy stopped and listened. He knew the nest was there. There had been one in the barn every year since he could remember. But he had been forbidden to climb and look, since the nest was high and dangerous, and barn owls attack when their young are threatened.

"Weird noise, isn't it, Dad?"

"Ay, it is that. Never forget the night your mother first heard it. Carrying you, she was. She heard that snoring and thought we had tramps in the barn. Yelled out to them to clear off, else she'd get the police. Then that big 'un, old Barney I suppose it was, he gave a screech and swooped down and nearly frightened your mother to death. An' you as well. She swears those owls had something to do with you arriving a week early." Sam Holdern gave a laugh as he clapped his son's shoulder. "Fact was, I thought you was an owl the way you yelled. Horrible noise, you made, just like that bird."

Chuckling, the two made their way to the house, the snoring persisting behind them. To different ears, those of Barney returning with Tyto's next meal dangling from his claws, the sound was the most pleasing in the world.

Barney landed on the beam beside the nest, a field vole in his grasp. This time, instead of tearing off the head, he pummeled the skull to pulp with his beak. Waddling along the beam, he gave it to Tyto. With a grunt, a pause, a shift in position and a final heave, Tyto swallowed it whole. His graduation to adult meals was complete.

While the chicks were small, Strega had brooded them with her warmth and protection. But Tyto had never stayed long beneath her wing, and, as the heat wave persisted and there was no danger of cold, Strega sat with them on the nest less and less. The times she was not hunting, she roosted on the beam alongside the nest, often with Barney beside her.

So the days and nights passed and turned into weeks. The heat wave broke and the drought ended with rain that brought a world of new smells and scents to the nestlings in the barn. On the first night of the rain, Strega flew out on the longest flight she had made for twelve weeks, since she had laid the first egg. She flew without purpose, not hunting, not searching, simply reveling in the rain that rippled through her feathers to her dry parched skin, flooding her with a new lease of life. Stooping and soaring, gliding and skimming the trees and the wires between the pylons, she celebrated the end of long weeks of brooding.

Behind her, Barney flew up and down anxiously, not understanding, keeping her just within sight, torn between his wish to fly with her and the need to stay within reach of the barn and his young.

Strega turned at last and soared over a cornfield. Her shadow across the stars caused a young field mouse to sit up and sniff the air quickly. Its life was over before it left the ground, gripped in the steely talons of its killer. Satisfied, Strega winged silently back to her mate and family. She gave the mouse to Tyto, the biggest and always the hungriest. Tyto swallowed it without even crushing the skull.

August went out with the rain still making up for its prolonged absence weeks before. On Sam Holdern's farm, the crops kept watered during the drought by dint of much effort were golden and ripe. The rain destroyed almost a third. The remaining two thirds were harvested at the first break in the rain and, at the end of the first day's harvest, Tyto left the nest for the first time.

Strega and Barney were not there. They were out in the early dusk on an orgy of killing, catching the scurrying, bewildered voles and mice left unprotected and uncovered by the cutting of the crop. The hedgerows were filled with rodents hunting for spilled grain, for holes and for cover. Tawny owls, little owls, even day-eyed kestrels took part in the frenzied hunt. Screaming swallows and martins dived and gorged on the clouds of disturbed insects; foxes, stoats and weasels slipped along the ditches, killing more than they needed. It was the autumnal slaughter, the night of the first day's harvest, a ritual none of the creatures knew as a ritual but as regular as the rising of the moon and as old as humankind's tilling of the ground

Perhaps it was the electric fluttering of the hunted insects flying into the barn that night which sparked the urge in Tyto to try his wings. Whatever it was, something prompted him to hop further along the beam than usual, right out over the hay bales. For the first time, he could see out the front of the barn, into the night; he could feel the uninterrupted wind from the world outside ruffling his feathers.

Tyto opened his wings to full stretch. The air breathed on the feathers, giving them a buoyancy he had not felt before. He hopped gently, testing this new-found lightness. Another step and his feet left the beam. A desperate panic-flap of wings, and then he was gliding, light and silent and as confident as Time, out of the barn and up on a tiny air current to the top of the cow shed. A few seconds there, then his deliberate wingbeats took him over the field and around to the barn, to land heavily on the roof. Next time, he would land more gently. It was all a matter of practice. He could hear his brother and sister chicks chittering and hissing hungrily below the roof. With a flap, he was up and soaring into the barn, where he landed on the beam, causing the three owlets to clamor for food, thinking he was Barney. Tyto stayed there, on the beam, preening his wing feathers proudly.

2

The Kill

With every passing autumn day Tyto grew stronger, and his flights took him further and further afield. The other owlets were soon following him, and by the middle of October all four were quartering the fields their side of the river as far as the woods and the common at the end of the village. And yet, so far, none of the young birds had caught their own food. Even Tyto, now fifteen weeks old, was still fed by Barney and Strega, who would find him, guided by his hissing call, and pass over a vole or a mouse or a young bird, which he would swallow voraciously. Tyto soon established a favorite perch, and every night he would wait in the dead ivy-clad oak above the farm lane for his parents to bring him their offerings. In the ditch below him, he would often detect shrews either by their rustling and squeaking or by the gentle movement of the grass and bracken. But so far he had made no attempt to catch one. That moment would come soon enough.

Until it did, Tyto was learning how to put to use the unique physical characteristics that perfectly equipped him as a nighttime hunter. His eyes were larger than those of day birds so that they could receive more of the available light, and, unlike those of other birds, both eyes faced the front. This gave him the binocular ability to see life in three dimensions, just like humans. Already he had discovered he could judge distances and movements better if he had several viewpoints, so while watching the shrews from his perch, he instinctively made the ducking, bobbing movements of his head which gave him this advantage. He was also able to see almost directly behind him without altering his position, merely by swiveling his neck. In this way, he could keep his wide-spaced eyes focused on a field of vision all around him.

The next night something new occurred. Tyto was clamoring as usual from his ivy perch when Barney flew from the wood and landed beside him, as he had a hundred times before. Tyto opened his beak with an anticipatory squawk. But Barney had brought nothing with him. He sat staring at Tyto as though at a stranger, and the young owl stared back. Then, to Tyto's dismay, Barney flew off, across the field and into the night.

Tyto waited. Out of patience at last, he opened his wings and launched himself in the direction the parent owl had taken. He flew across the field, then turned towards the wood. His wing muscles tiring, he came to rest in the fork of an elm.

There was a whirring of wings as he landed and another owl flew from the branches above. Strix, the tawny owl, indignant at being displaced from the vantage point he used every night, settled on a birch a few yards away and set up a low grating churr of resentment as he glared at the upstart. Tyto, uneasy and alarmed by the sound, took off again and continued the search for his parent. He was hungry. He had gulped down a chaffinch from Strega that morning and since then had had nothing.

Tyto flew over the top of the wood, uttering soft piercing cries, but he saw no sign of Barney or Strega. Then he heard the screeching call of a barn owl and turned towards it. He saw the bird near the river, soaring upwards, then dropping to land on the roof of the boat-house belonging to one of the riverside chalets. He followed and as he neared he saw it was his sister chick, Hessa. She squawked when she saw him, hoping to be fed. It seemed as though the owl parents were neglecting their duties to all their brood this night. Then, as Tyto flew off, he saw Barney swoop down and feed Hessa a vole. Tyto veered and flew after Barney back to the wood.

Barney ignored his call. The big owl descended and began quartering the hedgerow along the wood's edge, with Tyto trailing above him, croaking plaintively. The grass rustled and in one movement Barney tilted his wings and swooped, throwing out his feet at the last split second, and soared up with a wriggling harvest mouse. Tyto flew eagerly to his parent, who glided down to settle on the top bar of the gate through the hedge. Tyto settled beside him. Barney gulped down the mouse and took off, leaving Tyto with half-open beak. Uttering a cry that registered as much anger as dismay, Tyto again followed.

Barney flew slowly above the hedge. A frog hopped at the side of the ditch. A swoop and the frog was lifted in implacable claws. Tyto called in excitement. Then Barney let it fall to the ground, where it lay still. He flew off, leaving Tyto hovering above it. The young owl flew low, staring at the glistening shape in the grass, but he made no attempt to pick it up, slow to learn the lesson his parent was trying to teach. The owlet circled the dead frog again, grunting with hunger, then flew off over the field after his parent.

Barney had vanished again. Tyto saw no more of him that night but continued to scour the countryside in the vain hope of getting fed, his plaintive calls answered only by the mocking of the coots from the distant reeds and the hooting of Strix and his mate. Exhausted and hungry, Tyto returned to the barn to find the three other owlets already settling to their roost, replete and content. Of Barney there was no sign and Strega was roosting in the far corner of the roof, a new place for her.

Tyto pecked disconsolately at the casts on the ledge. The nearest owlet hiccuped a pellet. Tyto pecked at the tight wad of unwanted fur, bones, beetle casings and mothwings and rejected it. Hungry and puzzled, he hunched on the ledge as the dawn rose.

By midafternoon, Tyto could stand the pangs of hunger no longer. He hopped forward, stretched his wings and glided out of the barn.

The day was dull, with a light autumn drizzle that put

a glistening sheen on the russet leaves of the trees and hedgerows. Over the shining red roofs of the farm, Tyto winged his way across the field to the hedgerow where he had watched his parent catching food the night before.

In the field, Sam Holdern and his son were resowing the five-acre, the small farm's largest field, with wheat for next year's crop. Since harvesting in early September, the soil had been turned, the stubble ploughed in (Sam did not burn his stubble like some of the other local farmers) and with young John at the tractor wheel under his father's watchful eye, the seed was being fed into the straight furrows by the hopper the tractor was towing. Tyto veered as he neared the tractor, wary of the two figures who had stopped to watch him.

The boy shaded his eyes. "He's almost white, Dad, isn't he? Is that because he's young?"

The owl was silhouetted now against the dark wood and the contrast was startling.

"He's certainly whiter than any I seen before," said his father. "He's one of the young 'uns all right, you can tell by those downy feathers, and the way he's flying so awkward."

"Why's he out this time of day, Dad?"

The man shrugged. "Trying his wings, I expect. I dare say we'll be seeing some more before long. They've always had at least three young, my owls have."

Sam was proud of being the owls' chosen host for successive broods year after year. He had formed quite an affection for old Barney, and his son was even more fond of the birds. As a small boy, after his mother had put him to bed, John Holdern had many a time drawn back the curtains and, kneeling on the bed, had watched long into the night, fascinated by those pale ghosts flitting constantly in and out of the barn.

"I hope he stays, Dad, that white one. I like him. I'd know him again anywhere."

"Don't bank on it, son. Old Barney's young never stay more'n a few months. Like the young of everything else, they always move off, leave their parents. Like you'll be doing yourself in no time at all." He laughed ruefully.

The boy made no answer. His eyes were on the white owl skirting the dead oak in the lane.

Tyto had spotted the gate where his parent had perched last night. A vague prompting drew him to the spot where the frog had been dropped in the grass, but a hedgehog had snaffled that tidbit at first light. Without any definite intentions, Tyto, urged on by gnawing hunger and an indefinable impulse, began to imitate the behavior pattern of his parent the previous night. He flew low above the hedgerow, his eyes on the alert for the smallest movement, his ears attuned to pick up the slightest sound.

On the flight from the barn, Tyto's eyes had made a miraculous adjustment. The muscular iris, which at night expanded to allow all the available light to reach the sensitive retina, had contracted to prevent the excess daylight from blurring his vision. Now he could pinpoint even the long-legged spiders on the grass stems, and the ants as they filed through the leaves. But he saw no sign of a mouse or shrew or frog or even a beetle.

As Tyto reached the end of the hedge by the chestnut, a young greenfinch, harried by a bullying magpie, flew up from the hedge and all but collided with Tyto as the owl was about to descend. Instinctively stalling, wings out-

stretched, Tyto threw out his talons and ripped open the breast of the bird, which fell fluttering into the hedge.

There was a squawk from the magpie as he dived for the greenfinch and missed. The magpie half turned for another attempt but the sight of the owl deterred him and he flew off, chattering with rage. Tyto swooped into the hedge, heedless of breaking twigs, and seized the struggling bird in his claws. Flapping heavily, Tyto freed himself and rose into the tree. The greenfinch struggled for its life, but in vain, for Tyto's claws were grooved and the middle toes serrated, so that no prey could escape from their grasp. Then, just before landing, Tyto transferred the bird to his beak, where it was just as surely held. Tyto's upper mandible was almost straight and sharpedged, the lower one notched to give a better grip. Once on the branch, he lowered the bird and pinned it with his foot. A blow at the skull with his sharply curved beak, and it was dead. Tyto swallowed it and clucked with satisfaction. There was good reason for him to be satisfied. He had just successfully taken the most important step in his struggle for survival.

With each night that passed, the tendrils of November mist spread from the river further and further across the fields and into the woods. The protective canopy of leaves thinned and finally disappeared, compelling all the creatures who had hitherto enjoyed its shelter to exercise much greater stealth and caution. The pheasants and partridges crept furtively in the long grasses or stayed in the bracken; the hedge birds hid deeper in the tangled thickets; the mice and voles scurried for their lives each time they emerged from their holes. Some survived; some were sacrifices to the relentless cycle of life and survival.

Tyto and the other owlets quartered the district each night, hunting their own food. Strega and Barney hunted independently of them and the family was together only during the day, roosting in the barn. The nightly hunt was shared by the increased families of other predators— the little owls, the tawny owls, a brood of nightjars— while during the day, more kestrels, jays, magpies, and crows than ever before took their toll of rodents and small birds. There was even a lone buzzard, strayed from far off hills, who had found the pickings of the area to his liking.

Tyto very quickly found a quarter he preferred above all others, the stretch of riverside between the lockkeeper's house and the boathouse of the private chalets a mile upriver. By far his favorite prey were the rotund, furry water voles, which he snatched night after night from the star-flecked water as they nosed their arrow-rippled way between the reeds. Tyto soon perfected a hunting technique that was richly rewarding. It was to fly above the bank, with his head cocked sideways to the river so that his eyes could see every ripple and his ear cavities, though hidden by feathers, could pick up every sound vibration within their range.

And their range was far-reaching. Tyto's ears, more sensitive sonar-detecting devices than man had yet been able to imitate, were twice the size of his large eyes and could pick up the vibrations caused by the impact of a leaf hitting the ground. So keen were these sensory scanners that Tyto could detect the high-pitched calls of rodents and even of insects, well beyond the reach of human hearing. When he had located a swimming water vole, his form, on fringe-edged, velvet-pile feathers designed for silence, would appear unheralded, and many a vole never knew how death had reached him.

It was along this stretch of river that tragedy first struck the family of Barney and Strega, though at the time it did not seem a tragedy at all. Pila, the elder of Tyto's sister chicks, seeing Tyto lifting his third vole from the reeds and flying to the bank where he liked to eat his prey, decided to try her own skill further downstream. She had no sooner reached the willows when her eyes and ears detected a movement in the leaves. There a robin fluttered helplessly among the lower branches over the water. A silent swoop, and Pila flew to the bank with the robin in her claws. Behind her the willow twig snapped, making her start. She raised her head, revolving her agile neck to scan all around for danger, but there was none. She killed the bird and bolted it. A pricking in her beak caused her to wince with pain, but another gulp and the bird went down. But the pricking persisted.

Three hours earlier the robin had been caught the same way, impaled on a maggot-baited hook at the end of a fisherman's broken line, snagged in the willow. After snatching at the tidbit, the robin had hung, helpless, his life's strength ebbing. The claws of the owl brought merciful oblivion.

Now Pila, too, had the prong of the hook immovably sunk in her mouth. An angry scratching with her claw only drove it in further. Grunting with annoyance, Pila flew back to the barn, where her attempt to rub her beak on the beam succeeded in driving the hook deeper still.

Tyto, completely unaware of his sister chick's problem, swallowed the second half of the vole and flew back towards the boathouse. He rose and dived at the rushes, no longer hunting, but enjoying the shower of ice-cold dew spray he splashed from the stems as he passed. A moorhen screeched in alarm and dived, causing a circle to spread through the reedbed. On Tyto soared, upwards and over the field and, because he was fed and the half-moon was bright and no danger was there and owl life was good, Tyto let out his first screech, a life-cry of raucous discord that froze the blood of the scores of creatures who heard it but brought an answering scream from a brother chick three fields away. The two owls met minutes later over the copse and together they flew full of night joy on wild white wings to their birthplace to roost.

3

Escapade

The autumn mists sharpened into billows of frost and December winds took the last stubborn leaves from the trees with howls of triumph. Crusts of ice formed around the rim of the pond on the common. On the high slopes of the distant downs, the frost was thick enough to keep the imprints of the feet of feeding birds until midday. To Tyto, his nightly hunting flights were visitations to a new and different world. The land was brittle and the sounds made by the scuttling creatures carried further, confusing his sensitive ears. A dark shrew scuttled over the white starlit path. Tyto caught it easily and landed a yard from where he caught it, swallowing the still-moving corpse in seconds, then lifting himself on silent wings to the cover of an elm.

Hunting was still easy. From the elm Tyto flew towards the river. A water vole, browsing yards from the bank, froze for a second before racing for the water. Tyto caught it as it dived. The vole struggled frenziedly and Tyto, quickly and by instinct, for he had never yet needed to do this, swiveled the outer toes on each of his feet to become second hind toes. Now, instead of his usual grip of three toes in front and one behind, he had two at the back, and his gripping power was strengthened. Powerless in this grasp, the vole gave up the struggle and was dead before the owl descended to the boathouse roof. Tyto tore the head off and devoured it. Then he gulped the body and sat there with the tail protruding from his beak before that, too, was swallowed.

For an hour, contented, Tyto remained on the roof with only his head moving, swiveling and bobbing. He was almost startled into flight when a dog fox leapt on a roosting pheasant in the hedge near the boathouse. For several seconds, there was squawking and the cracking of twigs but the jaws of the hunter remained implacably locked and the squawking ceased. His prey limp in his jaws, the fox ran along the hedge, across the path and into the wood. Tyto, his head turned half-circle, watched the trembling twigs which told of the animal's direction and relaxed the muscles he had tensed for flight, content to stay where he was while his body pleasantly absorbed his night's intake of nourishment.

His silent vigil served another purpose. Simply by remaining there, he could build up a mental picture of everything that moved within a radius of a hundred yards or more. He could see the distant ripples of the water voles, the moorhens, the chub snatching a floating berry. He could hear the squeaks and rustles of the mice in the grass and the shrews in the ditches, the thud of rabbits sending warnings in the hedgerow two fields away. Had he still been hungry, the mole that pushed the frost-crusted earth from the burrow in the ditch would not have lived another minute. But what finally prompted Tyto to leave his post was not potential prey.

A barn owl, another male, came from across the river. Tyto saw him light on the pylon in the middle of the field. The owl then spotted Tyto and took off and flew noiselessly to the willow fifty yards upriver. Tyto shifted uneasily on his feet. A strange, unfamiliar hostility flowed through his veins. An owl was not food. This one, as yet, was not even showing aggression. But something told Tyto it was a threat, and he, too, took off, heading for the willow.

The owl stayed where he was, on the low branch, watching Tyto's approach. It was of no significance to either of the two birds that they were sprung from the same parents, for the stranger was Gar, one of Strega and Barney's brood the previous summer. Now well over a year old, the bird had returned from the village where he had, that year, mated and helped to rear a brood of two chicks, only to have his mate and both young destroyed by mindless village youths. Distraught and bereft of the company of his own kind, the solitary owl had come back to the place of his birth. But there was to be no welcome for him.

Tyto, in flight, raised the feathers of his crown and

hunched his head back while flexing his legs forward, a
sure sign of aggression and potential attack. The sitting
bird rose and flew from the tree, heading back across the
field. Tyto stooped at the fleeing bird in a mock attack.
To Tyto's surprise, Gar turned and responded aggressively, flashing upwards, showing his claws. Tyto swerved
to avoid a collision and he now became the pursued. Gar,
being older, larger and heavier, was much the stronger
flier, and three times Tyto avoided a slash from his talons
only by swerving. Back over the boathouse they flew,
and then, as though recalled by a sudden summons inaud-
ible to Tyto's ears, the pursuing owl turned and flew back
to the willow. Tyto, wearied by the strenuous flying,
landed heavily on the familiar roof. Fifty yards away, the
other owl settled on the branch. After recovering for a
few minutes, Tyto took off and headed to the pine trees
on the edge of the wood. As he flew into their darkness,
rabbits below him scudded for the safety of their burrows.

Tyto stayed in the pine till dawn began to rise. When
he left the tree, he flew in a sweep towards the river,
looking for the owl. There was no sign of Gar, so Tyto
headed back across the fields to the barn, over territory as
familiar to him as his own plumage. That flight across the
river had been his first venture there. Without his being
conscious of it, the experience had been a turning point
in Tyto's life. It had made him aware for the first time of
the significance of territory. An instinct, hitherto un-
tapped, had flooded through him at that first glimpse of
the stranger. The bird, as a male of his own species, was
not a friend, but an enemy. By its very nature it would
seek the same food from the same source of supply, and
was a threat to Tyto's survival, even though, at the mo-

ment, there was food enough to go around. Instinct governing his behavior, Tyto had seen the intruder off. In doing so, he himself had invaded the stranger's own hunting ground, and in turn had been driven back. The two rivals had ceased hostilities when the river divided them. From this night on, the instinctive recognition of territorial rights was to grow in Tyto to a point beyond resistance.

Back in the barn, as the dawn sun softened the night's frost, Tyto settled to roost beside his sister chick. Pila had not fed that night, nor for several nights previously. The hook inside her mouth had festered and now it was too painful for her to open her mouth. Hunger was weakening her and constant clawing at the source of the pain had created an open wound down the whole side of her head.

Three nights later, when Tyto returned before dawn, more than satisfied with his night's catch of five mice, a water vole and an injured young rabbit he had killed and only half eaten, his attention was caught by the unfamiliar movement of something on the straw-littered floor at the entrance of the barn. Turning from the beam where he was about to settle, Tyto swooped down and frightened off the Holdern family's tabby cat, which was tugging the dead carcass of a bird. The body was that of Pila, her suffering finally at an end. She had succumbed to weakness from hunger and fallen to the floor, dead even before the cat had found her.

Tyto soared back to the beam, his curiosity satisfied. The lifeless husk of skin and feathers had meant nothing to him. When the cat made its stealthy return and ran off with the carcass in its mouth, Tyto eyed the animal disdainfully without stirring.

The next night the weather changed. The wind increased and brought the first scattered flakes of winter snow. Tyto made his first capture without even leaving the farm. As he flew from the barn, he snatched at an incautious starling as it moved from its roost in the eaves of the farmhouse to join the other starlings in the cowshed. Carrying the bird, Tyto flew to his favorite vantage point on the boathouse roof, only to find that Gar was there before him, perched on the roof as though he owned it.

Startled and disturbed, Tyto flew past the owl to the other end of the roof. He had no sooner landed than Gar attacked. Tyto was so taken unawares by the viciousness of the assault that he made no attempt to fight back. He rose clumsily, only just avoiding the full force of the aggressor's beak savaging his breast. As it was, he lost a scattering of feathers and the dead starling fell from his grasp, sliding down the roof to the ground where it lay until discovered by a keen-eyed crow at dawn. Tyto, meanwhile, flew for his life. Gar pursued him with harsh cries and several times Tyto was buffeted in mid-flight by the stronger bird's wings.

Tyto instinctively flew to the barn. As he neared the familiar buildings, two owls flew into view and came to attack. Strega and Barney, their sensitive ears having picked up the owl-hate on the night wind, came now to defend their territory rather than their young. They did not discriminate between the invading disturbers of the peace. Both Tyto and his assailant became the objects of the angry attacks of the two adult owls. Tyto, repelled by Strega's threatening cry and display, flew past the barn and on over the farm. Behind him, Gar was chased back across the river, where he landed once more on the willow to be left in peace by his two ruffled, angrily chittering pursuers.

With his instincts and normal behavior pattern totally confused by this new experience, Tyto flew on and on over territory new to him, over thatched cottage roofs and the slates of the schoolhouse, over the village green and the pond, his wings aching with fatigue. When the dark tall shape of the church tower blotted the stars ahead, Tyto flapped his way wearily to the ledge of the bell-tower window. There, his breast heaving, his wings drooping as though weighed down by clay, he sat, hunched, bewildered, lost.

It was half an hour before Tyto recovered sufficiently to take an interest in his surroundings. There was blood on a few of his breast feathers where his attacker's first onslaught had scratched the skin. Tyto preened the blood away with his beak. The cut was not deep and did not pain him.

That done, he turned around and hopped through the opening into the bell tower. Inside, it was like the barn in appearance, though the smell was entirely different. Two giant beams crossed the tower from wall to wall. From these hung the three half-ton bronze bells upon which six changes were still rung as and when the occasion demanded. Strange creatures, birdlike but not birds, flitted around the tower with continuous high-pitched squeaks which jarred on the owl's sensitive ears. Then he saw one of the creatures cling to the walls beside the beam. Tyto opened his wings and pounced rather than flew, his talons sending a shower of dust from the wall as they closed on the prey. A clumsy fluttering of his wings in the confined space took Tyto back to the beam, where he pecked at his prey, already dead in his grasp. A gulp, and Tyto swallowed the bat, whole. The size was disappointingly small but he relished it nevertheless. Minutes later, another bat landed on the beam almost within Tyto's reach. A hop and jump and the second flying mouse disappeared. Tyto hunched himself comfortably on the beam, his memories of the barn replaced by satisfaction with his present situation.

For three days and nights Tyto took advantage of the plentiful supply of food, supplementing the diet of bats with the wood mice that scurried among the gravestones when the light had gone. Such easy pickings, such a safe, warm, dry shelter, were all that any owl could want.

The Sunday dawn rose like the others. But as the morning wore on, doors slammed below Tyto's roost in the bell tower, and the sound of voices carried upwards. Tyto shifted uneasily, then tucked his head down.

About a quarter of the congregation had arrived when the three Merford bell ringers, sweater sleeves rolled up and rosin on their palms, together pulled the ropes for the peal which summoned Merford to Sunday prayer. A ton and a half of tuned bronze crashed harmonically in the tower and sent the call across the thatches and the smoking chimneys. In the topmost rafters, the hanging bats shuddered at the resonance but slept on with accustomed unconcern. On the beam the barn owl, head wing-hidden, felt the sound waves strike not only on his ears but at his very nerve centers, paralyzing him almost to the point of death. Numbed and frozen and with no command over any of his muscles, the shock waves rebounding off the walls around him, Tyto fell and fluttered like a stricken moth down from the belfry, his fall interrupted only when

he struck the rafter above the bell ringers' heads. Still unable to regain his balance, Tyto tumbled to land at the feet of the men.

Startled and confused, the men forgot their practiced pulls and the matins peal became a discord that stopped Merford in its Sunday tracks.

Tyto floundered on the floor as though in his death throes, with no wits or instincts left. His threshing claw tore at a trousered leg, ripping both material and flesh. The man, his yell transmitting fright as much as pain, dashed to the door to escape to the church. Even in his fear, Tyto's instinct led him to light and air. Before any of the men could act to stop him, Tyto fluttered out into the church.

The open space restored his power of flight. Driven by the shrieks of the women, Tyto flew to the altar. A brass chandelier, bearing a ring of electric lights, hung above the steps. Tyto tried to perch on the ring. The chandelier swung alarmingly and Tyto lost his balance. His wings sent a light bulb down to the stone floor to burst like a grenade. In panic, Tyto flew to the pulpit. There the perch was steady and he paused to recover his breath. One of his pinion feathers, broken in his fall from the tower, wafted to the floor. By now, some twenty people were on their feet, shouting and calling advice to each other.

The verger approached wielding a broom. A thrust of the bristles sent Tyto tumbling from the pulpit, but he recovered and flew across the church. Now he settled on the rail of the organ loft. The organist was seated on the stool only three feet away. She clutched her throat as Tyto's head swiveled around and his huge dark eyes stared straight into hers. Tyto, startled, opened his beak and let out a squawk of fear. The organist sank onto the keyboard in a dead faint, sending a dissonant chord out into the church.

Tyto, spurred on by new alarms and new fears, now sought haven in the bright green trees below the blood-red sunset in the royal blue sky. His body hit the stained glass window with a crash and the face of St. Bartholomew beneath the fig tree broke into a smile. Half stunned, Tyto fell to land on the altar. One of the vases holding floral decorations crashed to the ground and a candle, spitting fat, flew like a comet to the altar steps.

By now, all the doors and windows that could be opened had been opened. As the cold December wind swept through the church, displacing the warm air, Tyto recovered sufficient of his senses to enable him to fly to the source of the welcome new scents. He flew over the heads and the waving arms to the porch. There, with the owl only yards from the open churchyard and freedom, the verger in a last desperate display of leadership before his flock took one more swing at the bird with the broom. Tyto evaded the moving broomhead with a lift of a wing. Its course unimpeded, the broomhead flew onward until it struck the side of the head of the trousers-torn bell ringer with an impact that rendered him insensible.

The assembly, by now silent and stricken with awe, watched the great white shape of the bird—or was it a demon spirit?—winging its way noiselessly over the gravestones towards the poplars bordering the churchyard.

"I know that owl," said a voice, that of John Holdern. "He's the big white young 'un from the brood at our farm. I'd know him anywhere."

Oblivious to the watching eyes, Tyto flew painfully in

among the bare twigs of the poplar and landed heavily on a branch. He was bruised and shaken and had slightly dislocated the forearm bone as well as breaking a pinion feather, but he paused only a moment. A greater need than recovery was the need he felt to put distance between him and Merford's inhabitants. He took off again and continued across the fields until those watching his departure could see only a small speck of white against the gaunt December sky. Then that, too, was gone.

4

Winter

Tyto flew erratically, taking no special direction. He became aware of dull pain in his injured wing, and of a smarting on his leg, where a candle flame had scorched him. He flew until not even owl eyes could discern the church tower below the horizon, and it was the longest flight he had ever made. The land below was new and strange. The tall Scots pines on the skyline beckoned him, promising shelter.

A sudden whir of feathers past his head made him swerve, startled. A chaffinch, one of a flock feeding in the hedgerow, took exception to the unfamiliar intruder. The bird was joined by others and the flock, incensed beyond any natural fear, dived and stooped at the hapless owl. Out of his natural element, flying over unfamiliar territory, the owl posed no discernible threat to the smaller birds, and the birds sensed this with a certainty born of instinct. They challenged the owl as of right and the owl put up no resistance. This was Tyto's first experience of mobbing and, following so soon after the other disturbing incident, his consternation was complete. Harried by the tiny aggressors, he fled to the protection of the pines, where he settled at last in the cavity under the torn bark of a broken Scots pine. The fallen trunk, still leaning, formed a spacious dry shelter and here Tyto welcomed the shade and the chance to rest.

He remained in the pine for the rest of the day. The sun disappeared behind clouds soon after he settled and the wind increased. Clouds gathered and the stars were hidden. It was after midnight when Tyto stretched his aching wings and flexed his cramped claws. He rose and glided from the branch.

He had not flown far when he realized that the night, too, always so reliable a friend, was changing character. Soft ice-feathers settled on his eyes and when he turned into the wind, stinging flakes drove him to turn again and fly with it. Snow was something else not within Tyto's experience. Baffled and alarmed, he fled back to the pine.

The blizzard continued until dawn, when the wind suddenly dropped. Tyto, who had expended most of his energy in the previous twenty-four hours, felt a desperate need for food. He ventured again from the tree in a silent swoop over the land beneath, only there was no land. The gray dawn strip along the skyline was reflected in a white mantle that transformed the familiar to the unfamiliar. Tyto, completely without bearings, flew over the changed countryside, frustrated in his hunting because there were no recognizable hedgerows or ditches to quarter.

Then Tyto spied the river, a gray dawn snake rippling furtively between white banks and snow-capped reeds. This was something familiar, and Tyto headed for it with relief. He saw the vole long before he realized it was a vole, a hopping brown dot on the white bank. He snatched it up in a burst of snow. The nearest trees were too far for the hungry owl, and he settled in the snow by the riverbank. There he swallowed the vole in three pieces. The snow around was flecked with red and dark fur. Tyto remained there, digesting, feeling his strength beginning to return.

A disturbance on the opposite bank caught his attention. A tall gray bird, difficult even for him to see against the snowy rushes, had a wriggling fish in his bill. Tyto had seen herons before, but never one so close, and never one that promised food. Tyto rose unhurriedly and flew across the river. The fish, an unwary bream caught feeding in the shallows, wriggled desperately in the pincers that were crushing its life away. Tyto stooped and buffeted the heron with his wings before the heron even saw him. Instinctively, the big bird resorted to his natural weapon, but in raising his spearlike bill, he dropped the fish. The bream splashed back among the weeds, floundering, mortally wounded. Again Tyto stooped but this time the heron was ready. The snake neck hurled the spear forward and Tyto escaped being impaled only by stalling a feather's breadth short of the point and diving sideways. The owl rose again but the heron's eyes were on him, and Tyto had had enough of unfamiliar encounters. He flew back to the other bank and settled on a snow-topped tree stump. Opposite, the heron langorously picked up the twitching fish, and this time the fish disappeared down the bird's gullet. For a long time, the two birds sat motionless, eyeing each other across the water.

Tyto was the first to move. The snow was numbing his feet, which he shook before he stretched his wings and rose above the sullen water. The heron stiffened, but no attack was forthcoming, and the tall bird relaxed to blend again with the kindred reeds. Like a great molten snow-flake, Tyto caught the golden dawn rays as he soared across the white field. As he flew over white hummocky gorse, a lapwing broke from cover and ran to the next white hummock. Tyto stooped and his first impact sent the large cock bird tumbling in the snow with a squawk and a puff of feathers. Tyto rose, turned and struck again, and this time his steel talons curled into the back of the bird. It was the largest prey Tyto had ever attacked and the weight was too much for him. Reversing his outer toes to give strength to his grip, Tyto dragged the bird along the ground, feathers and blood churning the snow. The plover turned its crested head to look at its attacker, and the owl's bill put an end to its struggling.

To Tyto, the dead weight felt heavier than before. Clumsily, he tried to fly with his prey, but he could not advance more than a few wingbeats. He let it drop and rose, instinctively looking for his favorite perch, the boat-house roof. But the boathouse was five miles upriver and Tyto had no way of telling where he was. He descended again to the corpse.

Tyto gorged himself until his crop was full. He perched

on the carcass, hunter triumphant on his trophy, and digested. Later he took off and leisurely made his way back to the pines on the hill crest.

That night it snowed again, and next day the frost arrived, crystallizing the soft canopy into glistening ice, so that the trees and bushes chinked in the wind and Tyto's feet crunched on the covered boughs when he landed. At dusk, when he returned to the plover's remains, he found nothing, only the feathers left by a vixen who had discovered the prize at midday. What she had not eaten there and then, she had carried away to her hole in the ditch and buried for later consumption.

Tyto quartered the field and the river. In the corner of the field, beneath two willows, a moorhen scuttled for cover beside the pond. Tyto glided overhead, his eyes penetrating the gloom and following the bird's movements through the dead nettles.

Tyto fanned silently above the undergrowth. The moorhen emerged and made for the reeds. Tyto stooped. The bird ran, across the water. Tyto, sensing something was wrong, could not pull out and grabbed with outstretched claws. But the moorhen had reached the end of the fringe ice and dived below the water. Tyto, who had landed in water before when catching voles, found this water was different. It was hard and solid and painful to encounter. His claws struck the ice and the ice shattered with a crack that terrified the owl. His wings beat in panic and his feet broke free of the ice with a suddenness that made him lose balance, sending up a shower of powdery spray. The surface of the small pond heaved under the ice as though struck by a tidal wave. Seconds later, Tyto was up and away and the moorhen, unconcerned at the havoc it had brought about, walked daintily back up the bank to continue grazing.

It took Tyto an hour to recover. Never again would he dive into ice, and the next moorhen would not be so fortunate.

That night, Tyto was unlucky. The night creatures treated the frozen world with caution. Tyto missed a vole that jumped and twisted as he stooped, and after that all he saw were mice scuttling for cover and a weasel that crouched and stared as he flew over, hissing a warning. Tyto had not encountered a weasel before but something told him he would be wise to leave it alone.

Dawn found Tyto with his hunger unappeased. Habit sent him back to the cover of the pine, but by midday his hunger was so great he could wait no longer.

The land was still white and frozen and Tyto flew a mile before he saw a sign of life—a farm, similar to his birthplace but with more cattle and livestock. Cows were crowding in the yard near the farm, pulling at the hay the farmer had forked out for them from the barn. The snow was churned into brown slush. In the entrance of the barn, where the farmer had disturbed the haystack, field mice darted, gleaning the grain. Tyto swooped as the farmer's wife emerged from the back door to shake a tablecloth. Tyto let out a screech as he lifted a mouse into the air without faltering in his glide. The woman dropped her mouth and the tablecloth and called her daughter to come and see but when the girl arrived, Tyto was out of sight behind the barn.

He settled on an outhouse roof and gulped down the mouse. Without pausing, he took off and returned to the barn. This time the girl, with her nose pressed against the frosted windowpane, cleared by her warm breath, saw the owl clearly.

"Look, he's like a gnome with wings," she called to her mother, entranced. Tyto dived and lifted up another mouse. To the girl's excitement, he transferred the mouse to his beak and alighted on the barn roof in full view.

"Mummy, he swallowed a mouse in one go, I saw him. Mummy, come and see, quick."

But her mother arrived too late, for Tyto was gone, drawn by the racing of a young rabbit across the field beyond the cows. Three times Tyto dived for the kill and three times the rabbit leapt sideways in midair, evading the outstretched talons. On the third stoop, Tyto tore a wisp of fur from the rabbit's back but by then the animal had reached the gorse and was safe. Tyto circled and screeched his disappointment. He returned to the pines with his hunger only partly satisfied.

That night he fared better, and in the nights following. December gave way to January, and Tyto was content to quarter the territory he had made his own. Here no other barn owl disputed his right to hunt. A pair of tawny owls shared the copse behind the hill where he roosted, but he felt no urge to drive them away. A pair of kestrels quartered the river but not having Tyto's power of night vision, they were usually returning to roost when Tyto's twilight hunting began, and there was no competition between them.

Though Tyto was barely six months old his skill was developing quickly, along with his strength and stamina. Of his youthful down not a trace remained, and his size, if anything, was already larger than average, even for a male.

The white coloring of his breast feathers had become more pronounced and his buff pinion feathers had lightened at the tips so that, in flight, he looked almost pure white when seen from below.

His sense of sound location had developed phenomenally. When clouds hid every star and not a splinter of light could reach even his sensitive retinas, his hearing homed him in like an arrow on the mouse that scuffled, the rabbit that bounded. With his widely spaced ears, sounds to one side of him reached one ear before the other, instantly telling him the direction of origin. Quickly, his head would swivel around, thrusting forward as he flew so that both ears picked up just one more sound. Then down, down in a silent stoop and up, at the last second, throwing his talons forward at the precise source of the sound, pinpointed with unfailing accuracy. This way, in the dark shadow of trees on the blackest of nights, he would catch his prey without so much as a glimpse of it. Small wonder then that scuttling rodents froze, anxious to twitch not even a muscle, when the screech rang out of the blackness above them. A tiny claw slipping on a blade of grass was sound enough and from nowhere, from everywhere, death would snatch them up into the night.

It was February before the snow cleared, melting in a warm southwesterly that brought a spattering of rain. The fields shed their whiteness and lay glistening and water-logged. Dabchicks forgot which were pools and which floods, and for three evenings Tyto fed off little else, catching the foolish yearling birds in open shallow water with nowhere to hide, nowhere to dive. It was with a young dabchick in his talons that he flew to the pylon and found another barn owl, a young female, perched on the iron girder. The bird, watching Tyto, stiffened as he approached, then took off, wheeling off into the dusk with a low cry. Tyto, not pausing, veered after her, the prey still dangling in his grasp. No set purpose drove him, only an irresistible need for the company of the only bird of his kind he had seen for five weeks.

For twenty minutes the two birds flew, following the curve of the river. Tyto was not aware that the young female was Hessa, his sister chick. Something was stirring within him and he followed the female over the boathouse and above the field. Suddenly he found his bearings, recognizing every bush, every tree.

He slowed down now, for he was tiring. The dead dabchick, though no heavier than a water vole, was heavy after such a long flight. And there was no need to hurry. He could see the barn now, his birthplace, beside the twinkling light of the farm. It was as though he had never been away.

As he glided towards his familiar vantage point, the boathouse roof, another owl appeared, this one a male. It landed on the other end of the roof, eyeing Tyto with its head tipped to one side. The low grunt was familiar and Tyto answered with a hiss of recognition. It was Barney, his father. The old owl knew his own instantly and flew off with a screech. Tyto pinned the dabchick underfoot and tore at it hungrily.

5

Departure

The next day Tyto roosted in the barn where he was born, along with the two adult owls, and Hessa and Bur. At dusk, all five owls left the barn and went their separate ways, for, like all their kind, each preferred to quarter an area free from encroachment. As Bur separated from Tyto over the field, he gave a low cry; Tyto flew on towards the wood.

Bur, five days younger than Tyto, was darker in color and slightly smaller. He had remained at the barn since his birth and the uneaten prey of the rest of his family had often provided him with a meal, thus saving him from going hunting himself. Consequently, his hunting skills were less advanced than Tyto's, though his stoop and kill were effective enough when his prey was caught unawares. But his experience of dangers was less and this fact played a part in the events that were to follow.

Bur took a course that led him over the outskirts of the village. A mile further on lay the Park House Farm estate, a thousand acres of mixed woodland and open heath, where Bur had found easy pickings of the shrews that scuttled noisily among the bracken. The owner of the land, the chairman of a large advertising agency in London, brought his friends down on weekends to enjoy the shooting. To this end, he employed Jed Coulter as his gamekeeper to keep the pheasant stock in plentiful supply. Bur flew over the woodland, his keen eyes scanning the grass below for movement, his ears sorting out the medley of night sounds.

A cock pheasant chased a female noisily through the undergrowth. Bur swooped down, curious. He saw the birds running off and ignored them, his attention caught by the flutter of feathers in a tree stump just out from the edge of the wood. He dived, ready to kill, but at the last second refrained from throwing out his claws to grab, for the bird, a starling, was already dead. It lay on the stump, the wind ruffling the plumage giving it false life. Bur circled, mewing cautiously, stooped again, and this time decided to grab. His claws snatched at the corpse but before he could lift it and fly off, a wire sprang around his legs. The impetus of his flight threw his weight against the noose, and both of his legs snapped. Screaming with pain, Bur swung heavily backward. His head struck the tree stump, knocking him almost insensible.

He recovered his wits in an hour but there was nothing

he could do. His snapped legs held tight in the implacable wire loop, Bur hung head down through the long hours of the night, with the dead form of the starling he had dropped mocking him from the ground, only inches away. His agonized flutterings and screeches weakened by the hour, until the cold light of day found him unconscious. Jed Coulter reached him three hours after dawn and, lifting the wire, dashed out the bird's brains in case life still remained. Jed had been caught like that before, by a devious kestrel playing dead which had slashed his wrist. Pleased with his night's catch, the keeper reset the pole trap, using the same bait, which he was glad to see was untouched, and went on to his next trap. Pole traps were illegal but no official ever checked these woods and Jed's only concern was keeping down predators of every kind. Jays and magpies were his chief target, for they wrought havoc on the pheasant egg clutches, but in Jed's eyes, hawks and owls were just as bad.

Oblivious of the fate of his brother chick, Tyto pursued his hunt with great success. The milder weather brought the worms from deep down to the surface, warm beneath the thick carpet of last autumn's rotting leaves. There the worms were sought out by the perpetually voracious shrews and moles, and Tyto caught and ate his first five shrews before stopping to digest. An hour in the fork of the sycamore and he swooped again, his eyes and ears leading him to the invisible mole tugging at a worm beneath the carpet. The mole was swept up to a quick death in a shower of leaves and Tyto flew with it to a nearby gatepost. Instead of swallowing it whole, he tore it savagely apart, relishing the sport as much as the meat.

It was the first of many such nights of easy pickings, and the reserves of body fat used up by the hard winter's hunting were rapidly replaced.

A week later John Holdern, on his usual Saturday afternoon ramble with the new binoculars given to him by his father for Christmas, came across the "gibbet" that Jed Coulter had erected near the TRESPASSERS WILL BE PROSECUTED sign at the entrance to the private wood. His eyes glanced distastefully at the wire strung between the trunks of two birches on which Jed had hung the gruesome trophies of his trade as he saw it. A long-dead jay, two magpies, two gray squirrels, a rook, a stoat and a large golden white bird that stopped John in his tracks, his heart thumping. He approached the carcass and lifted the wing gingerly, dispersing a cloud of flies.

"Oh, no!" John stared, aghast, as his worst fears were confirmed. The bird was a young barn owl and the sight of the white underwing and the creamy-flecked downy breast feathers brought a lump to his throat. For several seconds John was certain he was looking at the corpse of Whitey, his favorite owl, which he protectively regarded as one of the family. Only when he stretched the stiffened wing did doubts, glad doubts, return.

Remembering the episode in the church—would he ever forget it?—John looked for the damaged wing and for the missing pinion feather. Both wings were complete and perfect. He knew then it wasn't the owl he called Whitey, though it was almost certainly one of the young from his father's barn.

The boy's anguish diminished, but not his anger at the keeper who slaughtered such birds and hung them up like public enemies—the birds that caught the rats that ate the pheasants' eggs and young, that killed the young of the predatory gray squirrels, that took perhaps one occasional pheasant chick for every hundred of these rodents that plagued estates and farms alike. John knew his father would be angry when he learned of this, for he valued the help of the barn owls. Ten years if it's lucky, his father had said a barn owl lived. A good deal less if it had many pole traps to contend with. The boy eyed the owl's remains and on an impulse gave way to his emotions. He ran to the tree and, heedless of the metal snagging his hands, he unwound the wire and hurled the line of corpses to the ground.

"I'd like you on that wire, Jed Coulter," he cried, panting. Then without a backward glance he continued on his walk, but he turned for home sooner than usual, unable to recapture his earlier enjoyment.

At the farm, the owl life continued uneventfully after Bur's death. But at the end of March a noticeable change took place in the adult owls' behavior, one that was to alter the lives of the two remaining young owls. Over several nights, Barney and Strega paid increasing attention to each other. Barney would pass Strega the prey he had caught without eating any himself. He would peck her bill and make strange soft cries and Strega would reciprocate. The two adult owls bunted the young owls off the ledge, so that Tyto and Hessa had to roost on the beam. The young owls, too, felt a new stirring in their blood. Tyto felt uneasy at his roost even though his hunger was appeased. He felt the urge to fly, anywhere, at any time, without knowing why. Finally the time came when he was given no choice.

Hessa had not returned when Tyto flew back to the

barn on a dawn pink with the promise of sun. Gliding into the barn, he was startled to be met by Barney, his disc of feathers puffed out making him appear almost twice his size, flying at him in a clear display of aggression. Tyto swerved to avoid the assault but the outstretched talons plucked a burst of feathers from his flank. Frightened and demoralized, Tyto flew to the ledge where Strega, his mother, crouched watching with an implacable stare. She hissed a warning at him as he landed. Tyto took the hint and took off again, but Barney followed, buffeting the bewildered Tyto so that he fell to the hay bales. Picking himself up hurriedly, Tyto flew out of the barn, with Barney still pursuing and harassing him across the field as far as the wood. Only when Tyto sought refuge among the lower branches of the trees did his parent give up the attack. Trembling and distraught, Tyto hopped anxiously from branch to branch as he heard the owl cries fade across the field.

Tyto made his way in stages to the top of the tree and stared in the direction of the farm. He could see the pale forms of two owls stooping and soaring in the distance. Hessa was being given the same unexpected treatment, the treatment normally meted out to a stranger or an enemy. Tyto flew in a wide arc over the field but he could hear the aggression on the breeze and he knew it would not be wise to venture to the barn again. With the daylight lighting up the sky and spreading through the trees, Tyto turned his back on the place where he was born, and set out on the long flight to adulthood and natural independence.

Tyto flew towards the hollow pine which had been his

haven for five winter weeks, following an implanted sense
of direction with unerring accuracy, helped by landmarks
still unmistakable although the texture of the landscape
had changed. The sun had now cleared the horizon, promising the warmest day of the year. As Tyto flew over the
road, a car slowed as the interested driver watched the
unfamiliar daylight spectacle of a barn owl crossing the
gorse-spiked common, the morning sun gilding the buff
wing coverts and the white underfeathers with a brightness that looked unnatural. Later, the motorist was to tell
of the bird he had seen which was more like an apparition,
as big as an eagle and glowing like a ball of fire.

Unaware of the spectator, for a car represented nothing
alive or dangerous, Tyto continued his flight. The night
shadows were visibly shortening beneath him as the sun
rose. Wisps of evaporating dew spiraled from gateposts
and holly hedges. On the ditch banks, wood anemones and
primroses were budding and the bright green shoots of
bracken curled across the floor of the wood. Tyto skimmed the trees and ventured now across the broad flat
heathland, with the river glinting like a silver serpent in
the eastern haze.

Suddenly, a small flock of large black and white birds
rose from the grass as Tyto's shadow crossed it.

"*Pee . . . wit! Pee . . . eewit! Pee . . . eewit!*"

The loud cries startled the owl and when the six birds
stooped at him in mock attack Tyto faltered and looked
for refuge. But the birds never once came close to him,
merely diving at him and stopping short, content to vent
their irritation by loud cries and aerobatics. Tyto flew on,
disregarding them, and the birds soon tired of the display
and returned to their feeding. Shortly after, a magpie rose

from a blackthorn, squawking aggressively, but after two halfhearted dives at the unruffled owl it gave up the pretense. Tyto was quickly learning to ignore the mobbing that his daylight flights always seemed to attract.

Tyto reached the edge of the heath feeling in need of a rest. He had flown four miles without a break. A pylon offered him a perch and he flew above the wires and settled on the iron gridwork. But the buzz and crackle of the wires through the insulators and the accompanying vibrations were unpleasant and frightening. Tyto left hurriedly and flew down to a hazel, settling on the topmost slender twigs which bent under his weight. As soon as he had hopped to a thicker branch, the linnets noticed him and set up a tirade of chattering abuse, surrounding him with prancing anger and noise. A pair of yellowhammers flew from the gorse, and even the shy wren joined in, so that the owl was given no peace.

Tyto stayed there, however, his eyes closed, apparently immune to the din. The small birds which at any other time would be in fear of their lives fluttered insolently only inches from him. When Tyto's fatigue had worn off and he made to leave, the birds scattered. The owl stretched his wings and left them chattering vainly at their victory.

In twenty minutes, suffering from the exertion and the unaccustomed warmth of the sun, Tyto came in sight of the pine-clad hill where he had sojourned four weeks back. His wingbeats quickened as he neared the goal that past experience had taught him was a territory he could call his own: it had no other owl intruders, a hunting ground he had made familiar by quartering, and sufficient prey even in lean winter times. The owl expressed his pleasure at arriving with a screech that rang through the quiet pine grove.

In the water tower the other side of the trees, two roosting barn owls shifted uneasily as the sound vibrations of the distant cry reached their sensitive ears. The male even took a step towards the opening of the aperture between the massive concrete tank and ledge which had been their roost for four nights. The female blinked her eyes slowly as Tyto's screech registered within her but she made no move. If there was another male in the territory then the males would make the moves, that much she knew. She closed her eyes lazily as her mate returned to his roost at the other end of the crevice.

The following dusk Tyto glided from the pines, eager for food. His flight had used up a lot of energy and he was ravenous. He had not reached the foot of the hill before he heard the challenging cry of another male barn owl. Startled, Tyto turned towards the sound. Never in the previous time he had spent in the area had his sovereignty been put to the test by another of his species. Tyto swept around the hill with his facial disc feathers puffed out to give him his most fearsome look. As he rounded the fir trees in the half light, a barn owl crossed the gap on the hillside. Tyto veered towards it, then turned and circled, puzzled. The owl was a female and not the owl that had voiced the challenge. This put the situation in a different light. Far from being sovereign of the area, Tyto was the trespasser, for a pair of his own kind had settled here. Tyto glided towards the tree where he could see the female perched. So far, he had not glimpsed the male.

The female was a yearling like himself, with prominent dark flecks on her breast feathers giving her a speckled look more like that of a tawny owl. Her head swiveled to look at him, her eyes luminescent in the shadow. Tyto flew to the branch above her and her head flexed around so that she was looking directly behind her. Tyto's grunts were answered by a soft mewing that sent a strange, unfamiliar tremble through his body. In that second of time, Tyto's maleness asserted itself in every cell of his body, and his purpose in life was never again that of a young owl seeking only to hunt and survive.

When the challenging cry of the male rang through the pine-black shadows, it was a different Tyto who screeched his answer. No longer trespasser, no longer immature, no longer undecided, Tyto flew out to combat for a mate as well as territory.

6

Brila

The two owls knew each other instantly. Tyto recognized the bright orange facial coloring and the thick tarsal tufts of the owl he had fought on the boathouse roof. And Gar recognized the young owl he had already chased and dismissed. With a confident screech, he swept towards Tyto, eager to repeat his earlier success.

The initial confrontation was a testing. Both birds, now well matched in size, flew headlong on a straight collision course, stalling within inches of each other at the last split second so that only their wing tips met. But the second stoop was in deadly earnest, and they collided in mid-air, judging the impact to a nicety, each seeking with claw and beak to injure the other. The air was filled with the thudding of wing-beats, harsh angry cries and a storm-burst of feathers. Locked in combat, the two birds tumbled over and over in the night air down to the long wet grass where they rolled and squawked, stabbed and scratched, sending up a spray of silver dew.

Then, as suddenly as the fight began, it was over. Tyto's flailing claw found a hold on the flank of his enemy and Gar's skin was lacerated deeply. Letting out a croak of pain and chattering with rage and defeat, Gar broke free of Tyto and, blood running down his leg, the older owl beat a hasty retreat over the field. Relentlessly Tyto pursued him, but his aerial buffeting was mocking more than damaging. Behind him, a silent witness to the rout, the female, Brila, flew on a wavering course, anxious to keep both owls within sight and sound.

Once again the river was the boundary. Gar, diving and swooping to avoid Tyto's stronger pursuit, flew low over the rushes seeking cover under the hanging willows on the far bank. With a final sharp screech of victory, Tyto turned away and winged slowly back to the wheeling Brila. When he reached her he acknowledged her with a low cry, then both birds returned to the pines. Tyto landed heavily, exhausted but unhurt, while Brila swooped below the tree to snatch an incautious shrew. She took it to the next tree to devour it.

For two hours Tyto did not move, except to preen his ruffled feathers. Then his hunger drove him out again across the field. The sight of the river earlier had sparked a memory of successful hunting, and he headed there again, registering familiar landmarks. He reached the willows and the reeds. There was no sign of Gar. Two male water voles squeaked in angry combat as they fought,

writhing in the water-filled cattle hoofprints on the mud-
bank. Tyto dived and lifted both animals in his talons.
One, struggling, fell back into midstream, where it dived
immediately. Tyto landed on the water tower and smashed
the skull of the other with his beak. He swallowed it par-
tially and sat with the tail limp from his mouth. Minutes
later, it was gone. A lift of his wings and he was off again,
sealing the fate of a field mouse at the foot of the tower.

Long before dawn, Tyto's hunger was appeased. His
last catch, a young rabbit, was left half eaten in the lane.
Brila had already returned to the roost in the water tower
which she had shared for several nights with Gar. Although
the two had shared, the season had not been ripe, the
winter cold too recent, for Brila to have responded to
Gar's halfhearted attempts at courtship. No doubt, if
Tyto's arrival had not disturbed things, she and Gar would
have mated.

For Brila and Tyto, the mating urge which grew
stronger as the spring nights passed was outside their experience. Both birds being young, their courtship owed
nothing to mimicry or imitation of their elders. The unfamiliar urgings awakening in Tyto were from the dawn
of Time. Through him, Nature took its course, haltingly
experimental, unhelped by confidence.

His awkward posturings whenever he approached Brila
were rebuffed with sharp pecks, and her feathers rose
aggressively. Yet Tyto would not accept these signs of
antagonism from her as he would have done from any
other barn owl. When on one occasion he approached her
and she retaliated by fluttering and sparring with her
talons, he did not retreat. Instead, he responded by acting
aggressively himself, lowering his head, dilating his facial

feathers and thrusting at her with his bill. Since Brila was an inch or so bigger than he was, he would have come off badly had a real combat developed, but apart from angry clacking of her mandibles as she parried his thrusts, the hen bird made no attempt to attack.

The two owls shared several roosts, sometimes the tower, sometimes the hole Tyto had used before in the dead Scots pine, and one very warm night they roosted in the canopy of ivy in the fork of a giant elm. Each night they quartered the countryside within a two-mile radius. There was no need to seek further since the food supply was plentiful. Gradually, it seemed to Tyto that Brila's rejection of his attention was becoming less determined.

Tyto persevered in his immature courtship. In the peak of condition, he was handsome, though his first real adult molt was yet to come. His breast, exceptionally pale even as a fledgling, was now snowy white with none of the usual buff shading. His wings and back, amber-yellow shaded with ash-gray, were flecked with a striking pattern of brown and white markings. His broken pinion feather had fallen away, soon to be replaced by a perfect one, but the small dislocation would be with him for life and the gap was still there between the feathers. The broad soft feathers of his tail were again more white than yellow, barred with tawny brown. Gray and yellow featherlets formed a heart shape around the startlingly white down of his face, and his black eyes contrasted dramatically. He spent more time preening now, and was clearly conscious of his fine appearance, for his posturings in front of Brila took on a swagger of natural pride.

Brila, in contrast, was by nature less handsome. She was bigger than Tyto, but her plumage lacked the sheen of the

male bird. The whiteness was much less apparent, and her pale cream breast was edged by noticeable black flecks. Her back and wings were deeper in color, too, a rich buff with darker gray. To Tyto she was everything desirable, but already he had noticed her strange hunched posture and the fits of violent trembling to which she was subject.

Then on a night when the air was rich with the scent of pine and insects danced in frenetic clouds over field and river, the youthful courtship took another turn.

The quarter moon had risen when Tyto returned to the pine with a water vole in his bill. Brila was in the hole, huddled and silent. She gave a low cry as Tyto arrived. Tyto approached her step by step, and this time she made no move of rejection. Motionless, she waited until Tyto was beside her. His head made quick bowing motions and he shook himself, ruffling his feathers. He turned his face and rubbed it against the side of her head. She responded, bowing with him so that their faces stayed pressed together. Brila made a halfhearted peck at the vole but did not take it. Side by side, they sat uttering low cries, Tyto still with the vole in his beak. Then he stepped away, deposited the carcass on the branch outside and flew off, renewing the hunt.

The next night, Tyto repeated the performance, this time with no offering. Again Brila responded, snapping her bill and uttering a bubbling, chattering sound. Tyto, too, clicked his beak while he stretched his neck up and down as though trying hard to swallow. Both birds ruffled out their feathers as if putting on a display of aggression, and when Tyto began to sway his whole body from side to side, Brila followed suit. Now she was the one to edge

closer to Tyto and the clacking sound turned into a churring snore. As on the previous night, they rubbed their
heads together, lowering and raising themselves while
clicking their bills. Finally, Tyto did something he had not
done before: he stretched forward and seized Brila by her
neck feathers, shaking her from side to side. A loud squawk
from the hen softened quickly to a chatter of acceptance.
Well pleased with his reception, Tyto released her and
the two birds stayed together. When Tyto stretched out
his wings to fly, Brila followed immediately and the two
soared over the pines, scattering the midges, their shadows
freezing the shrew foraging among the pine needles into
petrified immobility.

Five nights later, as the fierce March gale blew itself out,
Brila flew back from the river after an unsuccessful foray
and settled in the tower roost. Tyto followed minutes later
with a field vole in his claws. He flew into the crevice
where she was waiting. For the eighth night in succession,
Tyto repeated his ritual display. Tonight he added something new. He raised and ruffled his feathers, then com-
pressed them again, repeating this many times. His manner,
too, was more aggressive, just as Brila's was more submis-
sive. When he stretched to rub heads, she took the vole
from his beak. Pinning it with a claw she began to devour
it. Suddenly, after loud bill clapping, Tyto seized her neck
feathers and shook her as though savaging a prey. When
he released her, Brila raised and lowered herself, uttering
soft plaintive calls. She was begging Tyto to mount her,
and Tyto did so. For several seconds the confined space
echoed with the loud beat of wings as he struggled to keep
his balance on top of her. Brila crouched, mewing, in total

submission as the two owls attempted to couple. But the coupling, doomed before it started, failed not only because of immaturity. There was a more deadly reason.

When Tyto stumblingly dismounted, he immediately began to preen his ruffled feathers as though nothing had happened. Brila's behavior was the opposite. She stretched her neck and preened Tyto's head feathers with her bill. Pressed side to side, the two owls mutually groomed each other, uttering soft cries. Tyto departed only because Brila was overtaken by a violent fit of trembling. Tyto always left her when she suffered these attacks, as though he could tell there was nothing he could do. Brila was slowly dying of poison.

Brila had been born in a cow shed, eight miles north of Merford. The shed was on the land of a farmer who had taken every possible precaution to safeguard his crops and his livelihood. He had liberally dressed the seed with dieldrin before the spring sowing, and when the crops were through, he had sprayed them with a solution containing DDT. Insect pests on his farm, the farmer intended, would never stand a chance. Unwittingly, he was meting out destruction to more than insects.

A small proportion of the spring seed was eaten by the usual seed-eaters, birds and rodents alike; the ground-feeders flocked, sparrows, chaffinches, greenfinches, linnets and pigeons; mice and voles scratched their way to some of the grain. Small quantities of poison went into the bodies of all these creatures. But when the young green shoots showed their heads and the crop spray was applied, much more damage was done. This deadlier poison, though it dispersed gradually in the soil, stayed as a protective coat on the plants. Every bud swallowed by the birds and rodents had poison still on it, a poison that stayed a very long time in all living tissue, scarcely dispersing at all. Every meal, every grain, added one more minute dose of poison to the amount already built up in their systems. To many it brought death, but to most of them it simply slowed their reactions so that they were the first to fall prey to the hawks and the owls. Poisoned rodents and birds, by the score night after night, week after week, were fed to Brila and her sister chick. The parent owls themselves were doomed to sterility and death. Now, a year later, the poison absorbed by Brila had spread throughout her body, finally reaching her brain, causing increasing convulsions.

Once the attempt at mating had taken place, Brila's earlier suspicion of Tyto vanished on the night wind and mutual affection grew up between them. The ensuing two weeks were spent in nights of easy hunting and days of companionship and trust. Often now, as the soft rains heralded the approach of April, Tyto would return to Brila in the water tower with an offering of food—sometimes a water vole, a shrew, a mouse, a frog, even a young gray squirrel. And Brila accepted everything eagerly, devouring it and mewing for more. She made hunting forays of her own less and less now and stayed huddled and disconsolate in the roost.

During the day, Tyto would sit close to Brila and they would groom each other with much bill-clapping and soft calls. Brila's bouts of shivering occurred more frequently and more severely. Sometimes she seemed to lose her balance and staggered, other times her whole body would shake in a spasm of pain.

There was one dawn, however, when their troubles were forgotten. Tyto returned from devouring a newly hatched coot he had discovered in the reeds to find Brila clucking in the corner of the crevice with unfamiliar excitement. Her first egg was laid. She nodded rapidly, drawing Tyto's attention to it, a small white sphere, sterile in any event, but now smashed beneath her tail where she had dropped it. The poison in Brila's system had caused an abnormality to the calcium formation of the eggshell so that it was paper-thin. With the yellow yolk of the life that was never to be spreading beneath her feet, Brila chittered proudly while Tyto hopped to and fro in excited satisfaction at the greatest feeling of fulfillment he had ever known.

For a night and another day, the two birds cherished the pathetic white object beneath the shivering, dull-eyed Brila. She laid a second egg, but this was even thinner-shelled and broke on emerging. Even Brila took no pride in this, for she clawed the mess away with desultory scratching. In doing so, she utterly crushed the first egg, and now the situation was apparent to both birds.

That night, the two owls left the nest and the broken remains, though neither bird felt any strong inclination to hunt. That part of Tyto which had been so completely fulfilled was now empty and frustrated. As he listlessly scoured the edge of the wood, it was as though he was hunting from habit more than the need to survive. Eventually, a snuffling shrew crossed a bare patch of ground and was snatched, killed and eaten in seconds.

Brila, too, caught a shrew, then a field vole, but this she left on the branch of the tree where she took it. Crying plaintively, she flew to where Tyto was quartering the field and followed him.

For the next week, the two birds went through the motions of their natural routine, roosting by day, hunting by night, in a lackluster, benumbed fashion. But as spring turned into summer, and the drawn-out evenings proffered plump pickings from the season's crop of new-grown creatures, the two owls responded to Nature's reassuring mood. At least, Tyto responded. Brila, whose shivering bouts had increased in spite of her recent renewal of appetite, began to get worse. In July, the birds tried mating again but Brila, in spite of Tyto's elaborate overtures, this time did not respond. She rejected him savagely, her instinct telling her she would never brood another clutch of eggs, and Tyto quickly dropped his attentions. As the summer wore on, she hunted less, until by August she was eating only the offerings that Tyto brought to her. Day by day Brila grew weaker, barely eating at all.

Towards the end of July, both birds went into the molt which owls and most birds undergo once the breeding season is over. The once-bright feathers, which had become worn and bedraggled from the ardors of raising their broods, needed replacing with new. In Tyto's case, true to his kind, the feathers fell in regular sequence over the next three weeks, his large wing feathers going first, not pushed out by the new growths as with some birds, but dropping like dead hair as fresh plumes grew alongside. At the same time as his wing feathers changed, so did his tail, the outside feathers falling first, the others going in sequence to the center until all the old had been replaced. Next, from rump to head, his body feathers dropped as new ones appeared. Bedraggled and half-plucked in appearance, Tyto's spirits were low during this time, and he spent the long days hunched unhappily and the nights embarrassed by his imperfect flight.

The molt took even more out of Brila, weakened as she was. For days she had not even eaten the prey that Tyto brought her. On a night in early September, when the first wisps of autumn drifted from the river at dusk, Brila did something she had not done for weeks. When Tyto flew from the tower to hunt, she followed at once, as though she knew that this night would be different. Taking off from the ledge, she spiralled almost to the ground before she could coordinate her muscles. Only at the last split second did she stall above the grass and soar in pursuit of Tyto's white form.

Tyto reached the river and found his favorite reed bed. Brila stopped, exhausted, in the willow. She perched on a branch above the flowing stream, her breath a hoarse croak in her throat. As Tyto swooped at—and missed— a diving water vole, a severe convulsion shook the whole of Brila's body. She died as she sat there, toppling slowly as her talons loosened their grip. Her fluttering form fell into the water. Tyto, thinking it another vole diving for its life, did not even turn his head. He never saw the sodden bundle of feathers swirl past the reeds and out of his life. Instead, his keen eyes stayed riveted on a young rabbit in the middle of the field and he winged silently to it. A scream, a second's frenzied kicking and the white wings rose and beat their way back to the tower.

There was no answering cry as he landed. Leaving the rabbit on the ledge outside, for it had been intended as a gift, Tyto called softly. He rose and circled the pines, then flew back to the river. Up and down, the white shape, now silver in the moon's light, now black against the stars, quartered the riverbanks for a mile each way. Back and forth to the silent tower, only the distant yap of a fox mocked his calls. He returned to the willow where the leaves whispered in secret, and across the black rippling water his screech echoed like a soul in torment.

7

The Search

For two weeks, Tyto continued to search. The pairing of his kind was meant for life, and although his mating with Brila had failed, the lifelong bond had been established that now was suddenly, inexplicably severed. Tyto was demoralized. No instinct guided him, no adult showed the way, only time and survival were the teachers. Gradually he came to accept the situation. He was alone again, with no mate, no eggs, nothing on which to focus his protective instinct, stronger now than at any season of the year. His unanswered screams echoing through the pines night after night became less and less frequent.

Tyto hunted alone in the territory for the remaining autumn months, sharing the abundant food supply with a family of little owls without dispute or resentment. There was enough for all. By day, a pair of kestrels quartered the fields and the fringes of the wood. Occasionally a sparrow hawk made a foray from somewhere across the river. Tyto's main diet was newly fledged birds and mice and voles, in which the area abounded. He had mastered to perfection the art of gliding at dusk over the hedges where the birds, young and old, roosted, and startling them with a scream that sent them scuttling for cover, so giving themselves away to a lightning pounce. He even took to coming out before the sun had set in order to catch the grazing field birds, lifting off unwary young peewits, larks, and meadow pipits and sometimes a young moorhen or coot chick that had strayed from the river.

Tyto had one near escape. On a warm September twilight, when the river was busy with the pleasure cruisers that churned noisily upstream and down in threes and fours as the locks divided the traffic, a boy with an air rifle saw him quartering the reeds and let fly. One pellet parted Tyto's flight feathers, another grazed his dangling leg. Not knowing what the danger was, only that there was danger, Tyto dived for the willow and hid till the boats had gone by.

Autumn faded, curled and died. The starkness of winter returned and Tyto faced it alone. This time, however, he fared much better than the year before. The winter turned out to be mild, one of the mildest on record, but what made the real difference was the increased skill of Tyto's hunting. Now he knew the signs, the giveaway clues of every moving creature; he knew when to hover and wait, when to perch, watch and listen, when to stoop and kill.

His skill did not go unobserved. On a night in January,

when the frost was tipping the grass with silver just before
the dawn, two anglers sat absorbed in the prospect of a
record bream when, as both had seen a thousand times
before, a vole nosed out through a willow's dangling
branches, heading for the other bank. It was halfway
across the stream when from somewhere behind the stars
swooped a great white wraith, snatching the vole up in a
burst of spray. Upstream they went, past the first of the
open-mouthed men, and the dangling legs of the owl
caught the invisible line from the rod. A screech of the
reel, a shout from the man, a splash as the rod was jerked
into the water; then the snagging of the line to let the
white wraith and its prey vanish over the reeds. All within
a space of two seconds.

When the men found their voices, their curses drowned
the clucking of the disturbed coots and moorhens in the
rushes. A night's patient ground-baiting was ruined, for
the turmoil would have scattered every fish for fifty yards.
Swearing vengeance on all owlkind, the men recovered
the rod and their shattered wits and made their way home.
Before long, their resentment began to mellow.

"We got no fish," said one, "but we got summat all
right."

"What's that?" the other queried.

"We got a fisherman's tale that'll see us all right in the
pub for a week or two."

The other laughed. "You're right there. It's a different
sort o' fisherman's tale, too." He paused. "This 'un's true!"

Unaware of his second claim to fame and folklore, Tyto
flew back to the tower with his catch. The men's shouts
had alarmed him. He had seen them there but had sensed
no danger, yet that snagging on his legs before the line

had slipped had frightened him and made him wary. Once in the seclusion of the roost, his calm returned and he feasted. His next foray was away from the river, which he avoided for the rest of that night.

The cycle of the seasons turned and the countryside responded; sap rose and filled the veins of the leaves; buds formed, opened, blossomed; hedgerows thickened; birds, animals, insects paired and prepared for young. In the tower roost, Tyto languished. Half his instincts were urging him to seek a mate, yet for some reason he was reluctant to leave. This was his territory, won in combat, where he had paired with a mate for life and nested. The influence of the season resolved the conflict. On a cloudy night, long before the March day was due to dawn, Tyto flew from the elm where he had landed to eat a mouse and headed back towards the tower. He had spent the last few nights calling in vain for a mate. He had heard or seen no owl of his kind since that September night when Brila had vanished. Suddenly, the need was so strong he flew over the tower and on, over the pines, and on, on across the dark starless land.

With very few rests, Tyto flew south until dawn. He covered six miles. Six miles of calling and still not a sign of another barn owl. He was now ten miles from Merford and the landscape was considerably different. This was much flatter, less wooded; it was arable farm land where the trees had been felled and the hedgerows removed in order to give clear runs for the mechanical harvesters and tractors.

Tyto looked for a roost near a village. He felt no nervousness at seeing people, for his first memory was of a farm and he knew rats and mice would be nearby. He soon found a hole in the side of a fallen oak, propped against another, and settled for the day, tired but content.

At dusk, he sallied forth to the red-roofed farm and the row of dutch barns. Rats scuttled in the straw. He caught and ate three before resting for an hour on the farmhouse roof. After hiccuping a pellet, he took off to continue his search.

He flew south again, pursuing his impromptu course of the previous night. After a few minutes, he became aware of a noise that was increasing beyond the level of any sound he had heard before: a roar deafening and stunning his sensitive ears so that he flew, terrified, for cover. Trembling, he hid in a sycamore as the monster passed above him. Gradually the skies quietened and the vibrations faded and vanished. He ventured out and resumed his flight, coming to rest on the roof of a low square building beside a vast open plain.

Tyto had arrived at an airport.

He stayed there for a while, uneasy at the unnatural flatness of the expanse in front of him. In the distance, the low roar of planes moving along the runways deterred him from attempting to fly straight across. Instead, he flew to the low bank of alders that edged the field, scattering a flock of roosting starlings. He settled awkwardly on the flimsy top branches. A movement in the grass caught his eye and he swooped, lifting a field mouse lightly back to his perch. A stab and the mouse was swallowed. Below, he could see other movements, hear other sounds. The field was alive with rodents. Unhurriedly, he caught and ate two more mice. His screech stilled the twitter of the starlings in the neighboring bushes, but only for a moment. Another sound reached him, a sound that froze

Tyto to the branch. It was distant, but his ears had caught it, just as the distant ears had caught his cry. Again the sound was repeated, and Tyto's wings trembled and shivered as he sat there. It was the call of a female barn owl, as unmistakable to Tyto as rippling water to a desert traveler. He screeched a reply and lifted himself from the alders, heading unerringly to the answering call. Half a mile away, in the fork of a hornbeam, Alba watched the distant white shape of Tyto winging his way towards her.

8

Alba

Tyto's courtship of Alba was very different from his wooing of Brila. Gone was the uncertainty, the nervousness of a new experience, which along with Brila's insidious weakness had doomed their mating from the start. This courtship was taking place between two fully adult birds. Alba was one year older than Tyto, and her mate of last season had been killed by a car soon after her brood of three chicks had successfully hatched. The death of the father had brought about the death of the two smaller chicks. With no mate to help her, Alba had hunted and brought back as much food as she could, but the largest chick, larger by five days, had grabbed all she brought. He had thrived while his fellow chicks starved. They, in their turn, for Nature's ways are practical, became food for the hungry youngster. Fully fledged, he had kept company with Alba through the winter, but a month ago had set off at dusk, never again to be seen by the parent bird. For a week Alba had scoured the countryside in vain. The young owl had gone for good, spurred on by his first spring fever to new territory, new allegiances. So Alba had wandered, hunting alone, calling to her kind, and finally arriving at the airport. Tyto's cry had set her trembling with aggressive and sexual excitement.

The courtship at times resembled a combat. Unpartnered for so long, Alba's instinct to mate was in conflict with her independence. As with all owl matings, the line between affection and aggression was gossamer-thin. The awkward displays that Tyto had tried out on Brila were now more deliberate, more accomplished. His posturing was like a trained ritual dance, and the castanet music of their bill-clacking rang out through the twilight.

The courtship began at their very first meeting, though only another owl would have seen it as such. Tyto's reception when he first arrived was distinctly unfriendly. Alba flew at him and chased him off with low cries and savage thrusts of her bill in flight. Tyto was prepared for this and retaliated. Alba's immediate retreat was significant, for it revealed at once that the hostility was ritualistic. Chasing her back to her perch, Tyto attempted to seize her with his beak. She fought him and prevented it, but when Tyto sat only a short distance away and made no move, she made no move either, except for a forward nodding of her head. By unspoken mutual consent, the two kept company for the rest of that night and the following day, roosting under the eaves of a derelict hangar on the edge of the field. Alba seemed unconcerned by the noise of the planes every hour, but Tyto was worried by it.

Next night, and the next, the courtship progressed. Alba accepted a field mouse, but she still brutally parried Tyto's attempt to get close to her. For minutes on end, faces only inches apart, they would nod and tremble their wings at each other. Alba consistently snapped her mandibles together, which Tyto took as a warning.

On the twelfth night after the first meeting, Alba's attitude changed. Her bill-clicking ceased; she seemed less antagonistic. Yet when he tried to close with her, she flew at him, knocking him fluttering from the branch. It was the moment of decision for Tyto and he took it. Angrily, he flew at Alba, who was not expecting it, and lunged at the feathers of her throat. His bill clamped tight, then instantly relaxed, for it was in his power to kill her. She responded by swaying from side to side and gradually Tyto released her. The natural aggression of two killer birds had, in some instant miracle of chemistry, been transmuted into just the opposite, a bond of trust fragile at first but soon to grow so strong it would unite them for as long as both birds lived. After she was released, Alba clicked her bill against that of Tyto, then flew from the tree with a chittering of pleasure.

Three nights later, amid the rubble of years of pigeons' nests on the ledge under the corrugated iron roof of the hangar, Alba and Tyto mated.

As the nights passed, the aggressive side of their displays diminished. Now they found pleasure and satisfaction in close contact, standing pressed together, mutually grooming and uttering soft cries. There was not complete har-

mony, however, for Tyto found it impossible to adjust
to the ear-stunning roar of the low-flying aircraft that
passed overhead every hour. Night and day the trees trembled, and the hangar vibrated with the crashing sound
waves that Tyto learned to dread. On his hunting flights
through the wood and over the field, he would sense the
approach of a plane and race for cover, terrified and deafened. Alba, who had been raised within earshot of another
airport some miles away, although temporarily deafened
in the same way as Tyto, did not appear to mind and
recovered much more quickly.

Twenty nights, however, were as much as Tyto could
stand. On the evening of the twenty-first, he made it clear
that he was anxious to leave. It was only his now unshakable affection for Alba that had persuaded him to endure
the area for so long. When the echoes of the last aircraft
had died away, Tyto flew out of the hangar and circled,
crying plaintively. Alba flew out to join him, uncompre-
hending. Tyto flew purposefully off on precisely the route
which had led him to the airfield. He flew for half a mile
before he turned and circled, calling with a harsh cry
unlike his usual screech. Alba, clearly disconcerted, answered from a distance, reluctant to leave the spot which
was to have been their nesting site. Tyto single-mindedly
flew on.

He flew for almost a mile before gliding down to rest
on a pylon. Below him, the headlights of cars flashed by,
crisscrossing on the six-lane highway with the sound of
a low continuous snarl. Alba was nowhere in sight. Tyto
called, a loud screech that went unheard by the motorists
but carried clearly to the soaring Alba half a mile away.
Her answering call put Tyto to wing and he flew off to

meet her. Wheeling in the sky, mewing and calling, their two white forms were lit up every few seconds by the car lights from the brow of the hill; spectral will-o'-the-wisps vanishing, reappearing, vanishing. Then away, together, the fine-spun bond now an intricate web of affection tying one to the other as they made their way to a new territory.

The course the two birds took was quite precise. Tyto's recollection of it was complete. He was leading Alba back to the water tower and the hunting ground that had already proved so fruitful over two past winters. In a short time Alba would lay her eggs, their eggs, and the parental instinct in them both, heightened after their first mating, drove them on when otherwise they might have dallied. They covered four miles and then, well before dawn, they stopped to rest in a tree Tyto had rested in previously. They stayed for two hours, each successfully catching enough to satisfy their hunger. Tyto caught two field voles while Alba heard the flutterings of a roosting flock of house sparrows in the ivy on the side of a barn and caught one before it could fly. Minutes later she returned and caught a second.

The spring dawn was breaking as they resumed the last part of their journey. Tyto's single-mindedness had proved infectious and now Alba, too, flew determined and eager over the changing landscape. For both birds it had become a flight filled with instinctive joy and excitement. With strong silent wing-beats, the two birds veered and swooped and soared in the first rays of the new day. On they flew, over the dawn-reflecting ponds and the gently billowing seas of grass, the stream and banks bright with coltsfoot and primroses, the green and yellow patterned celandines and wood anemones, the vivid green of cow parsley and the darker spikes of bluebell. March was turning into April and every living thing was jostling eagerly for room to grow and multiply. As the night shades melted westwards across the land, the rays from the eastern horizon gilded first the tops of the trees, then, moving imperceptibly, transformed the sullen droplets of the dawn into sparkling diamonds of light and life. The land glistened and shimmered, breathing mistily as the warmth increased.

From the nearby copse, the commuting rooks began their raucous journey to their feeding grounds, bundling past the two wing-weary owls in groups. One small party took exception to the aliens and stooped in mock attack but both owls ignored their antics and their cries and the rooks, deprived of fun, went on their way.

In the distance, the sun flashed from the river and Tyto called excitedly. A few more minutes and the pine-crested hill stood against the golden sky, the water tower beyond it.

As the two owls reached the pines, a bird flew out at them with an angry flight display, chittering resentment. It was a long-eared owl, who thought to nest among the pines with his mate, at that moment hunting far beyond the river. Tyto chased the indignant owl but without rancor. He was tired and he would deal with usurpers to his hunting ground some other time. Just now he needed rest. His excited chatter told Alba that their destination had been reached. With silent wings outstretched, Tyto glided to the familiar ledge. He jumped, startled, as a stock dove flew out from the crevice, its panicking wings brushing his face. On an untidy platform of twigs inside was the one white egg the dove had laid the previous day.

Tyto speared it with his bill and drank the contents. Alba shuffled in beside him and she preened the yolk from his bill with her own, uttering soft cries of pleasure. Side by side, their muscles weary and their hunger beginning to return, the two birds settled down to rest.

Alba laid her first egg two days later. Then, at two-day intervals, she laid two more. Three perfect fertile eggs, which for thirty days she constantly warmed beneath her. All that time, apart from flights lasting only minutes to stretch her wings, she was fed by the attentive Tyto. More food than she could eat accumulated on the ledge, where, fly-blown and inedible, it would stay until hurled from the ledge by one or other of the birds in a spasmodic attempt to keep the nest clean. Their casts and disgorged pellets accumulated and were scattered haphazardly.

On a day in early May when a sudden shower was pattering on the concrete, filling the cavity with echoes, the first egg hatched. Tyto, roosting at the far end, hurried forward at the unexpected cheeping cry. Apart from a quick glimpse of the naked, wrinkled chick when Alba stood up to remove the broken shell and egg sack, he did not see it again that day. But the pride was there in his flight that evening as he went into the dusk to find food, not just for his mate, but for his family.

Two days later the second egg hatched, and the third another two days after that. Three blind ungainly chicks, with their bulbous egg-teeth and ever-open beaks, clamored for food. Now Alba could help hunt and provide, and the lives of the two owls centered around nothing else.

The season was wetter than usual but for the owls this was to the good. Plants, buds and seeds luxuriated and rodents and young birds thrived, which suited the birds of prey. Tyto's way of life was now complete. This was what he had been born into the world for, the extension and continuation of his kind. His skill at killing was at its most refined, his aggressiveness at its peak. For the next two months of that glorious summer, Tyto lived out the purpose of his existence with the greatest satisfaction he had known.

In the hottest week of that summer, the two teen-age boys hitchhiking their way from London to the coast thanked the driver of the car who had given them a lift to the outskirts of Merford and walked towards the village. The hour was late, near midnight, and their packs were heavy. The Holdern farm's big stone barn, some distance from the red-roofed farmhouse, stood silent and inviting. The bales of straw promised a soft bed and the two hikers decided to stay. Within minutes they were in their sleeping bags, finishing their cold meat pies. In the morning, they would be gone before anyone knew they had been there. Above their sleeping forms, the two barn owls, Barney and Strega, were more silent than usual, anxious not to reveal the location of their eggs.

At dawn the two young men awoke, both cold and hungry. They had no more food or drink, and sat listening to the farm awakening around them. Packing up their things, they made ready to leave for the village where they hoped to find a café. As they left, both smoking cigarettes, one threw the lighted end away without thought. The first wisps of smoke did not emerge from the barn until the two were out of sight along the road. Sam Holdern with his wife and son were at their breakfast when the alarm calls of the scuttling geese took them to the window.

There was nothing anyone could do. The fire engine arrived when only the rear wall, of solid stone, was left. The straw, the beams, the roof, were heaps of smoldering ashes. Somewhere in them were the ashes of the owl they had called Barney. Both birds had stayed too late, in a hopeless defense of their eggs against the smoke, an enemy unknown to them. Strega managed to take off, but there was no way out save through the middle of the dense black fumes and she, too, like her mate, fell choking to her death. The boy found her charred remains beside the wall. Though now, at sixteen, more man than boy, the tears welled in his eyes.

"It took the owls as well, Dad, look. I wonder which this was? I wonder if old Barney got away?"

Sam Holdern shook his head. Even though he was more concerned about the insurance and his cattle feed, he shared the boy's loss.

"Doubt it, son. They'd stay by their eggs, see. They wouldn't stand a chance, not either of 'em."

The boy stared at the smoking ruin. "No more owls," he whispered. "No more owls at Holdern farm. It won't feel right. There's always been owls here, as long as I've lived!"

9

Evicted!

Five miles away, completely unaware of the tragedy that had struck at the place of his birth, Tyto and his family continued to flourish. The three chicks grew with astonishing rapidity. The short grayish white down had changed within two weeks of their hatching to longer, denser, almost pure white down. At four weeks old, their pinched, wizened faces smoothed and broadened out into facial discs much lighter in color, and the first feathers began to appear on the edges of the wings and tail of Ula, the oldest, biggest chick. At seven weeks, she was noticeably more advanced than the other two, a fact that was soon to stand her in good stead.

It was a sultry July day when the green van left the

distant highway and crossed the countryside on the narrow private road to the clearing at the foot of the water
tower. It was the annual inspection of their property by
the Water Board officials. The tower, built at the turn of
the century, had been out of service for thirty years. The
pumping station had been dismantled after the war, and
the tower kept as a landmark and a public memorial to an
earlier social service. Its upkeep was the Water Board's
responsibility, and once a year two officials came to inspect
this pleasantly situated, but otherwise quite forgotten
outpost.

Two men got slowly from the van and lit up cigarettes.
They were in no hurry. There was only routine work to
go back to, this outing only happened once a year and the
sun would be out shortly, once those rain clouds had dispersed. They chatted as they smoked, leaning on the van.
Then they took a ladder from the back. A metal ladder
was already fixed to the side of the tower, but officials had
removed a fifteen-foot length from the bottom in order
to prevent adventurous children yielding to temptation.
The men propped their ladder up to meet the metal one
and the first man began to climb.

He reached the metal ladder and transferred his feet. A
climb of a further ten feet took him to the ledge around
the outside of the great concrete tank itself. The ledge at
each corner was protected by eaves, forming enclosures.
In one of these was the nest of Tyto and Alba, now both
crouched tense and silent over their three chicks. The
knowledge of danger had infected the young birds and all
five sat motionless, listening.

The man began his cursory inspection of the outside
wall of the tank. The turncocks had long since rusted into

immobility, and all the pipes had been removed. He began to haul himself gingerly onto the ledge itself.

Tyto could stand the suspense no longer. The sound of the man on the ledge told him the danger was approaching. Walking to the opening, Tyto emerged only a yard from the man's startled face. Tyto hissed, dilated his eyes and puffed out his feathers, almost doubling his size. The man, preoccupied with negotiating his transfer to the ledge, was caught completely unawares by this sudden apparition. Letting out a yell of fright, his hands slipped on the concrete. Almost losing his balance, he clutched wildly at the metal ladder as his feet sought to find a rung. He slid halfway down before they found a purchase.

"My word, Tom, what are you doing?" his friend called from the foot of the other ladder, where he was holding it firm.

Then Tyto took off, flying straight for the unfortunate Tom. Holding on with his hands, Tom took his feet from the rung and let himself slide quickly down, unable to contain a shout of fear. His friend below yelled his warnings as the wildly thrashing feet kicked the wooden ladder almost from his grasp. Tom transferred to this, and continued down. Tyto, alarmed by the cries and thinking the danger more real than ever, resumed his attack. Claws outstretched, his stoop at the man's upturned face could have caused serious injuries, but the man took the wisest, promptest, if risky, evasive action. He released the grip of his hands and feet and slid the length of the ladder, his rapidly descending back catching his astonished upward-looking friend off guard. The two tumbled heavily to the ground. As they got to their feet, a screech sent them racing to the van.

Breathless and in a state of shock, Tom sat rigidly in the van seat, staring at his scratched hands, conscious of splinters in his legs. His friend, almost but not quite as paralyzed by the turn of events, looked blankly out through the window at the owl on the top rung of the ladder.

"My word, Tom, look at that devil. We could've been killed. That bird could have done for us both."

Trembling, Tom turned and stared. Tyto, still huffed and angry, lowered and raised his head challengingly.

"By heck, Alf," he whispered. "Let's get out of 'ere. I'm all shook up an' that's a fact!"

"If you say so, Tom. What about the ladder?"

Tom's short reply was to the effect that the ladder should remain where it was.

With his shaking passenger beside him, Alf drove off down the road. He knew a pub where his friend would benefit from some restorative spirit. Come to that, he could do with some himself.

From his vantage point, Tyto savored his victory. He watched till the van was out of sight, then returned to where Alba sat protectively hunched over the owlets. She mewed thankfully as he returned and Tyto grunted, satisfied.

A week went by and Alba and Tyto mated again. The first brood was nearly self-sufficient and the year was young enough for them to raise a second. On the night following their coupling, Ula, the oldest chick, learned to fly. The moon was full and the countryside was lit as though by daylight when she accompanied Alba to the willows by the river. There she sat churring noisily for food, which both parents brought her. After she had been fed, Tyto took food to the other chicks in the nest. He had become adept at snatching moths on the wing and some nights he would catch over thirty. These, along with cockchafers and beetles, and mice and shrews, formed the basic diet of the owlets. He and Alba fed chiefly on field mice, for this year the area was overrun with them.

Ula returned late from her flight, some time after dawn, and only then at the insistent calling of the parent birds. The roosting birds had scarcely settled when the green van arrived again at the tower. This time Tyto came to the entrance of the nest as soon as he heard the engine. And this time the same two men had come prepared.

The ladder was still in position. The men wore heavy coats and thick gloves, crash helmets and goggles. After delivering their report on the tower's unofficial and extremely hostile inhabitants, the men had been instructed to rid the tower of them and wire the nest site up to prevent any bird returning.

This time, Tom climbed the ladders determinedly, and waved his hammer at Tyto when the owl dived to attack. Reaching the ledge, he took out a torch and shone it into the cavity below the eaves. At once the nervous Alba flew at the offending light, which the man quickly withdrew. Ula, frightened by her parents' cries, flew out after her, flying awkwardly to the top of the tower where she settled, calling in alarm. Tyto and Alba soared and stooped and hurled themselves at the figure on the ledge, easily avoiding the swings of the hammer. The other man climbed the first ladder, carrying a stick and a sack.

"Two more little 'uns still in there," called Tom. "Give me the sack."

Undeterred by Tyto's hissing stoops past his head, Tom

reached into the cavity with his gauntleted hand. First one squawking chick, then the other was thrust into the sack. Only the second man prevented Tyto's claws from tearing at Tom's coat, so desperate and enraged was the parent owl. Alba flew in mock attacks, torn between her nestlings and the plaintive cries of Ula on the tower.

The sack was passed down to the ground. Now the hammer went to work, nailing wire over the opening to the nest. That done, Tom edged around to the other side and nailed wire over the eaves to block the second entrance. The two young owls were destined for an uncertain future as pets for the two officials' children, who had requested them if any should be caught.

The men retired to the van with the satisfaction of a job well done, and drove off down the lane. Tyto soared above the van for a hundred yards or more, then returned to the tower.

The three owls were distraught. It was midday and their nest site was impregnable. Tyto flew against the wire, tearing at it with his claws and beak, but all he did was hurt himself. The sun was warm and bright and already a blackbird had told the district that barn owls were about. Two missel thrushes rattled around his head in daring swoops and a jay scoffed derisively from the top of a hazel bush.

Disoriented, bewildered, Tyto could not settle. He circled, uttering a stuttering call, and flew towards the trees. Alba followed and, reluctantly, the frightened Ula.

They came to rest in a tall spruce in the pine grove. From the Scots pine nearby the long-eared owl clacked warningly from Tyto's former roosting place. The three owls huddled together where the thick foliage afforded protection from the sun and the mobbing birds. Only the persistent blackbird followed them into the dark pines, keeping up his monotonous alarm. Then he, too, gave up and flew off.

Tyto could not decide what to do. He left the grove, flew towards the river, then circled back towards the waiting owls. He knew they had to find a nest site, for Alba would be laying her second clutch soon. He returned to the branch beside her and began to preen his ruffled feathers. Alba hopped closer and helped him with his grooming. On the pine-needle bed below the tree, a young gray squirrel sat on his haunches and watched the owls with black bead eyes. He gave up his intention of burying a hazelnut shell and scuttled for cover.

That evening the sun slipped below the world's edge in a crimson fire. Perhaps it was this sunset that decided Tyto. When the day's last light was extinguished, the night stayed bright with myriad sparks of its own making, sparks that twinkled back from the shining holly leaves and the glistening lily pads that bobbed across the river. Inside Tyto a desire was kindled that grew quickly in intensity. Gliding from his roost with a purposeful screech, he flew directly westward, towards the vanished sun. Silently, above the river and the willows and beyond, he soared with Alba and the young owl following. For an hour, the two adult owls hunted and fed their chick and themselves, but it was clear that Tyto was anxious to be off. Restless, he rose, summoning his family with chittering calls. Alba flew towards him, the protesting Ula not far behind. Tyto circled once more over the reeds and the mud-trodden cattle-drink and willows that he knew so well, as though taking a last look before setting on his predetermined westward course. Behind him, now white, now black through the starcast shadows like giant moths in candlelight, the two owls followed.

10

The Journey

Dawn found the three travelers seven miles from the tower. The river, which had disappeared from their view several miles behind them, had made a wide sweep and was back in sight, glinting across the field from the ivy-clad elm where they had settled to roost. Somehow Tyto, whose survival from owlet days had been closely dependent on the life of the river, was comforted by its presence. He settled on the branch beneath the thick canopy of ivy and prepared to sleep out the sultry day that was already making its presence felt.

Early that evening, three hours before dusk, Ula left the roost and flew, crying hungrily as she quartered the hedgerows, as she had seen her parents do. Tyto and Alba watched, unmoving, from the elm. Nature's circle turned, and now it was Tyto's turn to pass on to his chick the lessons that Barney had passed on to him. Ula was going to have to kill for herself. The situation the owls found themselves in was, in fact, accelerating Ula's education. Barn owls did not normally journey long distances with their young. The eviction from their home was compelling the owls into unusual behavior. For three hours Ula flew up and down the hedges, screeching and mewing, glimpsing several field mice and shrews and once, a baby rabbit, which would have provided an easy meal for an experienced bird. All Ula did was swoop and hover clumsily above the startled creature, which took several seconds to realize its good fortune and dart to the nearest cover.

The darkness sharpened the appetites of the two adult owls and both silently drifted from the elm on velvet wings to the fields where the unsuspecting prey were feeding.

In seconds Alba had lifted up a field mouse from the long grass, and she flew with it to the low stone wall that marked the boundary of extensive riding stables. Ula flew to greet her with anticipatory cries, but to her dismay, Alba bolted it herself. Indignantly, Ula left her mother and flew off towards Tyto.

Tyto, fanning above the compost heaps in the stable yard, dived to a movement. With a sudden swerve he soared up, too alarmed to cry out, as a black cat, unseen even by Tyto's eyes, leaped from beneath a wheelbarrow. Tyto felt the rush of air from the claw that missed him by a feather's breadth and heard the hiss of disappointment from the animal as it darted back beneath the barrow.

The miss was as good as a mile and in seconds Tyto had

seen the straw trembling by the stable wall. A swoop, a grab and Tyto had a wriggling house mouse which he killed as he flew. Ula, who had witnessed her parent's narrow escape, and his catch, approached with hopeful mewing cries but again, when Tyto landed on the roof, she saw the prey being swallowed before her eyes.

Tyto, hardly pausing, lifted off and swooped as another movement caught his eye. The stable yard was alive with rodents. Again he caught a house mouse, this time a young one. He returned to the rooftop where Ula still waited, chittering angrily, and dropped the mouse, alive but mortally injured, on the tiles.

The mouse began to slide down the roof. Ula rose, beating her wings quickly, and stooped clumsily, mimicking a kill as the mouse slid to the gutter where it lay, twitching. Ula landed on the gutter, head bobbing as her eyes took in the tiny creature's every aspect. Tentatively, she poked it with her foot. The mouse stiffened in its death throes and, thinking it was escaping, Ula grabbed. Her claw, bigger than the mouse, enclosed it, crushing it. She lifted it up to her bill and crushed it even more, to pulp. Then she swallowed it. Tyto, chittering approval, flew off to feed himself. Ula had learned her first lesson well.

Tyto and Alba gorged themselves on the bounty of the stable yard while the young owl flew to and fro, seeking an opportunity to advance her new-found skill. A mouse scuttled across the damp, glistening cobblestones. Ula stooped. Both her judgment and her timing were a fraction off. The mouse scuttled to the cover of a compost heap. Ula landed on the cobbles and was already lifting off when the cat raced from its hideaway and pounced. Its claws tore into Ula's tail and the pain of losing several feathers drew a screech from her that shattered the straw-whispering peace of the stable yard. As she struggled to break free, Ula's beating wings buffeted the cat, which snarled savagely. Her fate was still in doubt when, plummeting silently from the night, Tyto thrust his talons into the arched back of the cat, eliciting a yowl that caused the horses in the stables to whinny and rear in terror.

For a second, the force of Tyto's stoop and upward lift succeeded in lifting the cat inches from the ground, but the weight was too much and Tyto unflexed his claws, releasing the caterwauling animal. In the house the other side of the yard, bedroom lights flashed on, spotlighting the cobblestone drama. Windows creaked open; voices called; a dog began to bark, shrill and excited. In the walled confines of the yard, the noise was bedlam; Alba, who had by now joined Tyto, chittered angrily as she helped to chase the howling cat across the yard. The stricken animal, in whose back eight small, deep punctures would remind him for weeks to come of this night's misadventures, streaked for refuge in an outhouse. Tyto let out a screech of triumph. In the stables, neighing horses panicked and kicked the doors in fear, the crashes echoing around the yard. The distraught Ula, mewing more with fright than pain, flew clumsily to the top of the wall, shedding one more tail feather, which spiraled lightly down to join the four already on the cobbles. Tyto and Alba landed beside her, where they preened and comforted her. Then the three owls took off, leaving behind them a scene of total confusion.

The man of the house, clad in a dressing gown, emerged with a double-barreled shotgun, loaded and cocked. As

he prowled cautiously around the yard, he was joined by two women, one on the verge of hysterics, and two children. The party peered around, totally bewildered.

"Whatever was it, Charles?" asked the tearful woman, trembling.

Her husband snorted. "Rowdy, drunken hooligans, m'dear, that's what. From the village, I'll be bound. Picked on the cat, by the sound of it, the devils. What with that and Rufus barking, it's got the horses jumpy—listen to 'em. I'll give 'em jumpy if I see 'em." He glowered around in the darkness. "A load of buckshot, that'll make 'em jump if I catch any drunk trespassing in here. Chief Constable'll hear about this in the morning." He turned towards the house. "Come on back indoors, the lot of you. They'll be miles away by now."

As the children followed their parents, the girl spotted a feather on the cobbles and picked it up. She stroked it, admiring its velvety pile.

"I do believe it's an owl's feather, Tim," she said to her brother. "That means there must be an owl about somewhere. Hope we hear it. I love the sound of owls."

Unmindful of the disturbance they had caused, the three winged travelers journeyed silently on. Ula's tail was painful but the flesh was not torn and her first molt, though not due to begin for some months, would replace all the lost feathers. Her flight was slightly less even and smooth but her progress at hunting, stooping and killing would not be seriously impaired. It did mean, however, that she found herself tiring more quickly and she could barely fly a mile now without a rest of several minutes. With that immediate recognition of an injury to one's own kind common to all wild creatures, Tyto and Alba were solicitous of the young owl's handicap. They rested with her when she stopped, and Tyto even called a temporary halt to his parental tuition of her hunting skills and fed her with a mole, which he watched erupt from the heaving soil-crater below the very branch on which he sat. Rested and fed, Ula took off and the three proceeded in this manner until well past dawn.

For the day roost, Tyto singled out a giant yew in the churchyard of the village they had reached. He was drawn to it by the dark protection it afforded, and he skimmed above the gravestones to its thick, seemingly impenetrable canopy. Ula and Alba followed and, landing on the low gnarled branch, they hopped up to the top where the gloom was perfect for a day of rest.

It was not to be a day of rest for Tyto.

For an hour the three owls dozed, recovering from their flight. The persistent cawing of the rooks on the other side of the churchyard was an inoffensive background sound, but in among it was a discordant note, a performer distressed and out of keeping with the rest. One of the fledglings of a second brood had fallen foul of the adult male in a neighboring nest and been attacked. Pecked and bleeding, he had fluttered to the ground and was calling for his parents. Unfortunately for him, his parents were a mile away, where half the giant flock had flown at first light to fill their crops with leatherjackets in the potato fields.

Tyto heard the distress calls and, his appetite still keen after a night of undue exertion, he could not resist the chance to investigate. He drifted from the yew and fanned above the gaping maw of the squawking injured rook.

He stooped and his talons grasped the bird, almost as large as himself. The young rook screeched in pain and fear of death and this time, at last, the rooks remaining in the rookery paid attention. There was a difference between an errant youngster bawling at his punishment and a fellow rook in trouble with a natural predator.

At the first terrorized shriek from the fledgling, the incessant raucous calling of the rookery's inhabitants ceased as though a switch had been turned off. But only for a second. Then, of one accord and in one giant motion, a swarm of rooks a hundred strong rose and in a swoop descended upon Tyto.

The sexton was the only actual witness, though the whole village heard the rumpus and wondered. The old man had just unlocked the door to his cubbyhole at the back of the church when he heard and saw his rooks, which he had known for fifty years, rise and fall like a black avenging angel. He could not at first see what had aroused the birds, but as he stood, shielding his rheumy eyes from the brightness of the early sun, he saw Tyto still clutching the young rook, and then saw the squawking black bird released; it fluttered to the ground not ten feet from him. The young bird was dying, its back torn open by the steely talons, its breast already pecked by its own kind hours before. In a quick reluctant act of kindness, the old man ended the bird's pain with a blow of its head against a gravestone. Then he watched the drama before him, and the old man's heart was with his friends the rooks.

Tyto sensed at once by the volume of the cries that this was no ordinary mobbing. He had been chased and harried at one time or another by almost every native member of the crow family, from rooks to crows, jays and magpies, even a jackdaw, but never had he suffered the combined onslaught of nearly a hundred birds. The crow kind were usually more playful than antagonistic, but it was clearly not so this time. The swarm descended towards him from their untidy treetop colony and Tyto flew for his life.

At first he tried to rise and fly over the church to the yew tree, but the first of the avengers were already overhead and the owl was forced to fly low, weaving between the holly bushes amid the gravestones, buffeted by half a dozen rooks as he did so. The man watching saw no escape for the owl and began to feel sorry for him. But Tyto knew that once he reached the yew tree he would be safe, for in the darkness under the dense foliage the roles would be reversed. There Tyto would be in his element, seeing where the rooks could not see, a silent defender armed with claw and bill able to hold an army at bay.

But it was touch and go whether Tyto would reach the yew. As he rounded the corner of the church tower, swerving to avoid the porch, the air seemed filled with wheeling black birds, cawing and shrieking in a piercing cacophony of sound that caused the old man, who came hurrying along the path, to put his hands over his ears. He turned the corner in time to see the white shape of the owl half walking, half fluttering through the grass towards the gnarled outflung arms of the giant yew. Now the sexton saw the owl's intention, and he urged him on. The owl had been taught its lesson, that was all the old man had ever wanted. He stood, watching with bated breath.

Tyto was almost exhausted. His head was bleeding from several cuts, and his body was bruised by rook-wing buffeting. He struggled, weaving and bobbing, through the switch grass at a level where it was awkward for the rooks to either fly or land. Under a barrage of beaks and claws and deafening croaks, Tyto blundered through the overhanging fringes of the yew, scattering a cloud of dead needles from the carpet on the ground. He fluttered upwards to a branch and, for the first time, struck back at one of his attackers who had ventured in after him, his savage peck drawing a croak of pain. In the brief respite that followed Tyto hopped up to the bough above, and the half dozen birds that had pursued him under the yew stayed on the ground, cawing in frustration. Higher and higher Tyto hopped, from bough to bough, until the birds below could no longer see him. Outside, the din of the rooks' resentment reached a peak. But Tyto no longer feared the din. He was safe, high in the thick green-black of the yew-tree's crown, grunting in reply to the welcoming chitter of Alba and their chick. The two waiting owls seemed unconcerned, puzzled by the din outside but not alarmed. Ula was disappointed at not being fed with a morsel of something and hissed her annoyance.

At the corner of the tower, the old man leaned and lit his pipe. That had been an interesting start to the day. He watched the wheeling throng still venting frustration around the impassive yew, conscious that in all his life, he had never witnessed such intense collective anger. He puffed a cloud of smoke, trying to picture the ruffled owl huddled in the tree, then walked back to resume his work. The raucous cries gradually began to diminish as the birds returned to their nests. Life, the old man mused as he

stepped among the gravestones, was never to be long de-
flected from its normal course.

It was midnight before Tyto ventured from the yew.
The old man's unspoken thoughts had been correct. A lesson had been learned. Never again would Tyto meddle
with any inhabitant of a rookery. He had waited till long
after dusk until the last of the rookery's evening gossips
had ceased for the night. There was a quarter moon, but
Tyto pushed through the foliage on the dark side of the
tree and flew in shadow until the church, the yew and the
roosting colony of birds was far behind. Alba and Ula
sensed Tyto's need for caution and kept close to him.

The moon's light revealed a rapidly changing terrain.
The flat fields and wooded pastureland gave way now to
more undulating heathland and the thick hedgerows became fewer, replaced by low stone walls. Tyto, whose
body was stiff and aching, had little appetite and even less
desire for the activities of hunting and killing. But he had
to eat, and seeing Alba and Ula glide off towards the hollow where already his keen ears had picked up the movements of rabbits, he followed slowly.

Within minutes Alba had caught a young rabbit, which
she took to a low stone wall and began to devour. Ula
settled beside her and shared the pickings.

Ignoring the warren in the hollow, for the kill would
have sent the rest of the rabbits to their burrows for a
while, Tyto skimmed the walls and a startled bank vole
scuttled among the stones. Fanning silently, Tyto waited
and when the vole reached the gap between the stones, he
dropped. Seconds later he landed, and the vole was swallowed. Up in a moment, to see what was rustling further

down the wall, he missed the tail of another vole as it shot into a hole. Knowing his reactions were a fraction slower than usual, he circled, chittering with annoyance, and headed back to where Alba was feeding. For the first time since his fledgling days, Tyto was glad to eat from the kill of another owl.

There was nothing left of the rabbit except a few splintered fragments of skull and bones when the three owls continued. The moon was bright, the wind blew more strongly over the gentle slopes and the shadows of the western horizon beckoned.

11

The Promised Land

The next three nights and days were without any un-
toward incident and the travelers made good progress. The
journey was somewhat longer than that usually made by
English barn owls seeking a territory of their own, but
traveling was no unnatural hardship for Tyto and his
family. Tyto's kind were accustomed to the *Wanderjahre,*
the "wander years" when, owing to a rodent famine or an
increase in their own owl population, they migrated far
and wide, even crossing the North Sea. To Tyto, the cov-
ering of distance was incidental to the discovery of an area
rich with food. Had he but been able to realize it, he was
making his task harder by responding to the urge to fly
westwards. This flight was taking him deeper into the

bleaker hunting grounds of South Wales and after an un-
rewarding night's hunting on the barren Brecon hills, the
next night was even less encouraging. Bare hillsides of
granite and slate, broken by the black hostility of coal
mines and industrial workings, forced the owls to fly during the hours of daylight. Their fifth day's roost they spent
in a giant spruce above a slow-flowing effluent-flooded
stream. Tyto, drawn as ever to the sound of water, had
hoped for voles and sedgebirds, but all the riverside creatures had long since given up and left.

In the early dusk of their sixth night they left the spruce,
hungry and dispirited, and headed into the warm west
wind, which seemed to carry with it promise of clean open
countryside.

They were not deceived. Two hours' flying, with unsuccessful forays after scuttling voles on gorse-covered
hillsides, brought them to an area of open country which
looked far more promising.

They had reached the beginnings of the reforested low-
lands, which stretched intermittently now to the far distant peaks of the north. The pines, of various ages and
therefore various heights, filled acre upon acre of the
sparsely-clad granite hills with somber greenness. In the
fold between the hills, the starlight shimmered on the surface of a massive new reservoir to which the pine trees
stretched. Tyto, chittering with excitement, led the other
two towards the gleam of water. There, surely, would be
the voles and dabchicks, shrews, frogs and mice that their
earlier waterside territory had provided in abundance.

It was not so. For an hour or more the three owls, unnaturally bright against the darkness of the still water and
the silent, sullen pines, flew up and down the mile-long

shore of the artificial lake and saw nothing. The icy water, dropping steeply to a depth beyond that of any natural river, was not the home of rodents and frogs. The narrow shallows did not suit the water voles. No mice liked the arid density of close-packed pines. It was a lifeless land and beyond the understanding of Tyto and his family.

Wing-weary and hungrier than she had ever been, Ula left the lake and flew to a granite crag on the hillside to rest. She settled silently and preened her tail feathers, where the pricking stubs of new feathers were beginning to appear to replace the ones she had lost. Then she called, hungrily, desperately, for her parents and for food.

Tyto, still unable to believe a land could be so bereft of wildlife, fanned above the black water, riveted by his own white moving reflection. Not even insects or fish disturbed the surface; only the wind from the hills furrowed it worriedly.

Tyto heard the plaintive mewing of Ula in the wind and flew towards her. He was conscious that Alba was coming to meet him over the pines. The two owls reached the crag together and their chittering calls revealed their mutual disappointment.

Alba settled beside her chick, glad of the respite, but knowing they would have to move on soon. Tyto made as if to land, but changed his mind and flew instead beyond the crag to the edge of the hill. His whole body lifted suddenly as he reached the rim, caught by the thermal updraft of the strong night air, and with surprise at the sight that greeted him.

The hill fell sheer for a hundred feet. Below him, the untidy rubble of slate slag glinted on the floor of the quarry, which had bitten a hole into the side of the hill. With his wings outstretched, Tyto felt the unusual sensation of falling slowly without having to move a muscle. Fifty feet above the ruined sheds, however, he brought his muscles into play so that he could control his glide. He needed to position himself for a killing stoop. He hung there, ready yet hesitant. The sight that greeted him was so unlike anything he had come across before that he was temporarily confused.

The floor of the quarry was alive with rats. They were everywhere, darting in and out, over and under the heaps of fallen, rotting timbers and the piled-up lumps of slate. The center of attraction was a shed packed with bales of hay, and as the creatures scurried to and fro their squeaking was like the babbling of a brook. Tyto hovered, bewildered by the evidence of his own senses, undecided where to begin. Lower and lower he drifted, a huge leaf circling from some hilltop tree, spiraling until the big male rat on the topmost piece of timber paused from cleaning his whiskers to sniff the air suspiciously. Seeing the rat was about to perceive his presence, Tyto stooped. His claws lifted the rat off the timber. Impatient with hunger, he landed immediately, killed the rat with a beak-blow and tried to swallow it there and then. The rat was large, too large for comfort, and with a gentle regurgitation, Tyto pinned it beneath a claw and tore it in half. Two gulps, and the rat was gone. Seconds later Tyto drifted from the timber and deftly snatched another from the grass. All around him now rats young and old, large and small raced for cover.

With the rat dangling in his talons, still alive, Tyto began the upward flight to the top of the quarry face. Again he spiraled, using the wind current that bounced strongly from the sheer wall, and with little effort arrived on the open hillside. Alba flew at once to meet him, her keen eyes spotting his success, and Tyto called his triumph. Now Ula, too, rose, mewing excitedly. Tyto hovered over the crag and placed the rat for Ula. He settled only long enough to crush the rat's skull, then he was up, calling to Alba. Together now, inches apart in the strong air current, the two owls flew to the edge of the hill and descended the long drop to the quarry floor.

The rats had reappeared from hiding and Alba grunted with excitement when, from ninety feet above, she saw the numbers. Wings outstretched, she glided swiftly to the kill. Behind her, Tyto snatched another. Seconds later, a screech reverberated from the quarry walls, diminishing until it was lost among the other sounds of the rustling, squeaking, scurrying night of plenty.

That night the rat population in the quarry was reduced by eleven. Gorged and content, the three owls sat on a rocky ledge and sleepily watched the gray dawn light move stealthily across the quarry. The weather had changed and a fine but penetrating drizzle came in thin-thick furls on the breeze, polishing the gray stone to a reflecting shine. The rats gradually retreated before the encroaching light, their own night feed over. Now they returned to the network of holes and tunnels among the collapsed and derelict worksheds.

The quarry, blasted from a hill on a sheep farmer's land, had been forced to close two years ago because the flooding of the valley for the reservoir had drowned the access road. Sheds, winches, winch-houses and a water tank had been abandoned and had succumbed to Nature's inexorable reclamation. Timbers rotted and collapsed; corrugated iron roofs dissolved rustily to flakes; the deep water tank crumbled and became fouled up with weeds and insect life, even an occasional drowned sheep. The presence of sheep had incidentally contributed to the phenomenal increase in the rat population. The farmer, whose sheep still roamed the hills around the reservoir, had with a weatherman's foresight stocked one of the quarry sheds with fodder for his animals. When the land was in the grip of winter and his struggling sheep hard put for food, he could walk the footpath from the farm and fork the fodder to them. The previous winter had been mild and the grain and fodder had been left untouched. This year had therefore been ideal for the rats, who grew fat and multiplied to almost plague proportions. Untroubled by humankind, they had been only rarely bothered by predators—the occasional buzzards, crows and hawks, marauding foxes and weasels, a pair of short-eared owls, which enjoyed an evening's easy pickings some two months back but had then moved on; it was not the hunting ground for owls. At least, it had not been till now.

From the ledge on the cliff, the big white owl launched himself silently and on one beat of his wings glided to the far side of the quarry where the timber side of a toolshed had crumpled against the rock, creating a mozaic of shadowed crevices and alcoves. Tyto landed and hopped into the shaded interior. It was a perfect roost. The splintered planks formed a platform against the bare rock and several layers of wood were jammed above, forming a strong protective roof. He walked out through another opening and hissed his satisfaction. The white forms glided through

the gray mist and settled beside him. Alba walked past him
and her excited grunts told Tyto that she, too, would be
content to stay. When Tyto moved up beside her, so that
their wings touched, she preened his feathers approvingly.
Here she would hatch the eggs she was ready to lay. Here
they would raise another brood. Ula mewed, resentful of
being ignored. When she moved too close, Tyto warned
her off with a sharp hiss. He sat, casually preening the
feathers of Alba's wing with his bill, contented for the first
time in days. Their journey was over; he had brought his
family to the promised land.

At dusk the next day, instead of leaving the roost to
hunt, Alba stayed on the ledge, listless and uttering frequent soft cries. Ula ignored them and flew off, but Tyto
lingered, his head bobbing as he sat by her side. But eventually he, too, left and soared across the quarry.

The day-long drizzle persisted, but to Tyto it was fresh
and pleasant. A movement caught his eye and he watched
Ula gliding to a ledge on the cliff with a rat in her claws.
Tyto drifted lower and singled out a big brown rodent
from the score or more that scurried to and from the shed
which served as barn. He watched it bob under a rotting
spar and reappear on the gray dirt; then he dropped.

The next rat Tyto carried back to Alba. When he arrived, he was greeted by a lively bobbing display and excited chittering. The first egg of the clutch glinted between her feet. Tyto dropped his prey and the two birds
bobbed and weaved, face to face, in a demonstration of
delight. Tyto flew out this time on buoyant wings that
stretched to the far ends of the night. Up, up, on the ever-

present currents caused by the winds meeting the vertical rock, and he was way above the quarry and the black rain-shimmering crags, soaring over land the like of which he had never seen.

Even in the darkness and the drizzle, his eyes could make out the circling horizon of black hills, and his sensitive ears recorded enough sounds to enable him to delineate the nature of the countryside in a way that a human would have found uncanny. He could tell by the swirling of the mist in the wind where the gullies and valleys creased the barren slopes; he could tell that no tall trees broke the wind's resistance, only the low-growing gorse and juniper and stunted blackthorn spreading from the hollows.

As he flew over this strange new territory, Tyto discovered that the air currents were even wilder and more random. Filled anew with the joy of parenthood fulfilled, Tyto soared, letting himself be carried where the night wind chose. Higher than he had ever flown, gliding longer and more freely, he ranged above the black slopes, an alien white spirit enjoying an exploratory visitation. The only bird sharing the sky was a night-black raven, croaking to the darkness as he sought his mate who had not returned as expected. The croaks faded downwind and then only the bushes whispered.

Later, his flight of elation spent, Tyto winged his way back to the quarry—his quarry, for the territory was his alone, to be held for his own kind against all other predators. As he sighted the jagged crag that marked the cliff edge, he saw the hovering white shape of Ula suddenly plunge out of sight. With increased wingbeats, Tyto headed after the young owl. He met her as she was flying to a ledge to consume the rat dangling in her grasp. She cried a greeting, which changed suddenly to a squawk of alarm as Tyto unexpectedly buffeted her aggressively. She landed and crouched, hissing defensively, but Tyto had turned away. He had made his point. Ula would not be allowed to remain with her parents much longer.

12

Unwelcome Visitors

August ran its wet and windy course and Alba sat brooding five eggs. With the food supply literally on their doorstep, Tyto caught enough food for both of them with less hunting effort than ever before. Because the food was so plentiful, he did not persist with his aggressiveness towards Ula, who continued to roost with them, though now she stayed a yard or so away, not huddled close as previously. On her hunting forays, too, she kept clear of Tyto, quartering that area of the quarry where there were fewer rats, but still plenty for her needs. These rats foraged for food away from the barn, among the rotting packing cases and ropes and empty diesel and petrol cans. Ula always managed to catch five or six a night as they scampered among the sparse grass and weeds, and by centering her hunting here she avoided arousing in Tyto any fear of encroachment.

It could not last. Tyto began to renew pressure on the younger owl as soon as the first of Alba's eggs hatched. By the time the fifth and last had hatched, in mid September, it was clear that real antagonism existed between the parent and the younger bird. In practical terms, there was no real need, for the food supply was as abundant as ever. The inroads made by the owls into the quarry colony of rats had been equaled by the new rats born, yet the instinct for preserving the territory's food for his new brood was so strong that Tyto attacked Ula with increasing savageness. It was an instinct that defied analysis, for no bird—in fact no living creature, not even man—could rationally predict the change of circumstances that lay ahead.

So the expulsion of Ula finally took place. For weeks now the young owl had roosted on her own, not welcome to share the nest-site. For several nights she had retreated warily from the threatening flights of the parent owl. In the gray September twilight when Tyto was joined for the first time in a month by Alba on a hunting foray, Tyto left his mate and flew to where Ula was quartering the entrance to the quarry. Usually, having chased her from the quarry, Tyto would resume his own hunting and ignore the other owl's return. But tonight he kept up the pursuit and the two owls soared, dived and twisted in aerial combat far out over the hills where neither owl had been before.

Two miles from the quarry Tyto ceased his harrying, buffeting flight and circled slowly, watching his offspring flying low over the hills further and further away until, like a minute blunt-headed moth, she dissolved into the twilit distance of a new and separate existence. Perhaps, among the images recorded in Tyto's brain, a memory flashed of his own expulsion by his parents. The screech that echoed through the rocky gullies as he wing-drifted back to his own kingdom seemed to have within it an unfamiliar note of sadness.

The next few weeks passed quickly for the quarry owls. With five ever-open beaks to fill, as well as their own, Tyto and Alba wrought havoc on the colony of rodents. By early October the pickings, while there in plenty, were no longer easy. The rats were wary now of the killers that had come to live among them, and their ways had changed. Rarely now did they cross a stretch of open ground; instead, they formed their runs from burrow to barn among the debris, covered and protected. For a while unwise young rats were caught with comparative ease, but soon a new generation was born into these dangerous days and was quick to learn from birth. The two owls soon required all their skills to catch a prey that was growing ever more wary. But catch them they did, and Tyto's largest-ever family thrived apace.

One tragedy occurred, with the irony of natural law. One of the chicks, the third to hatch and from the start the most venturesome, walked to the edge of the flat ledge that was the nest and toppled fluttering to the floor. It was midday, and Tyto and Alba flew distraught around the stranded though unharmed chick. At dusk, they brought him food and he swallowed the crushed baby rats with eagerness. Then the other chicks demanded attention and received their due. A huge male rat approached the owlet, which set up a chatter of alarm. A swoop from Alba sent the rodent instantly to cover. But the parent owls could only delay the inevitable outcome, not prevent it. More rats gathered at the sounds, and though they were sent scattering by the parent birds time after time, there came the crucial second when no owl eye watched. The chick was seized and dragged beneath a rotting plank; the owl became the victim of its prey. The distressed Tyto fanned above the spot, calling loudly, but a thin drift of feathers like thistledown was all he ever saw.

Life, the very next second, went on as before, and four chicks clamoring to be fed became the immediate and only concern of the two parent owls.

The days and nights passed and the chicks grew rapidly. But although the quarry paradise provided all their immediate needs, Tyto was unaccountably listless. Increasingly, the desire for a change of diet, or at least for a more varied diet, was growing within him. The food supply was certainly of adequate quantity, but in terms of the nutriment adult barn owls needed for staying in good health, a staple diet of rats was not enough. The diet needed to be balanced—by insect-eating shrews, by vegetarian mice, by seed-eating birds, by aquatic-feeding voles. After almost two months of living on the flesh of rats fed on grain and refuse, Tyto found himself seeking for insects, beetles, moths, even slugs and worms, though there were few of these about. Alternatively, he wandered further afield, either scouring the hills, or even quartering the unproductive reservoir, or visiting the sheep farm some four miles away. After that, the nearest human habitation was a small hamlet seven miles distant and too far for nightly forays.

Another cause of Tyto's unease was the ominous decline in the weather. The area was bleaker and more wind-

swept than any land he had ever known, but this alone was not the explanation. There was no doubt that, for October, the winds that swept in from the north were unseasonally cold. Tyto sensed this heralded a bleaker than usual winter.

The oldest chick was six weeks old and flapping its stubble-feathered wings when the first scene of the coming winter's drama was enacted. It happened in the late afternoon of a cold mid-October day. There was a flurry of activity among the rats in the quarry-floor debris. At first, Tyto paid no heed, but stayed motionless; only the sideways motion of his head revealed that his ear was missing nothing. Lately, as the accessible grain diminished, more and more fights were breaking out among the rats as they competed for the grain in the center of the rapidly reducing store. But when the shrill death-scream of a rat rang out, the owls stiffened to attention, every nerve sharpened. From the seclusion of the nest, they could see only certain patches of the quarry floor. But it was clear the rats were dispersing in a panic. Without being able to see, Tyto's hearing nevertheless painted him a clear mental picture of a larger animal among the rats—a long, slim animal that ran as fast as rats in and out of their runs, but could kill them with ease. Four rats died in quick succession. Then there was the sound of a body being dragged, followed by the crunching of jaws. But whatever the predator was, it was certainly not starving, for the sound of feasting lasted only a few brief seconds. The listening owls heard the creature run off across the quarry, out of even their earshot.

An hour later Alba left the nest to hunt, and Tyto followed soon after. This immediately set the chicks clamoring for food. For some days now, the adult owls had taken to quartering the more open side of the quarry, at the entrance. Away from the rock face, the gorse and scrub-covered land was more like the hunting ground they naturally preferred, and occasional rats were always wandering there. Alba spotted one at once and was already fanning over it when Tyto joined her. In seconds, both adults had a catch which they took back to the nest. The clamor of the owlets could be heard right across the quarry, echoing from the walls.

Five more rats were taken to the chicks within the next two hours and even they began to ease their cries. Now Alba and Tyto could see to their own needs. Together, they flew up on a spiraling zigzag course to the crags above, soaring in the currents of the night wind.

Even as they flew, both owls searched the ground below for prey. Though Tyto had, in all the time at the quarry, caught only one injured pipit on the hillside, he never gave up the hunt. Tonight the sky was clear, occasional clouds flurrying swiftly in thin drifts between the stars and the pale half moon. They quartered the hillside for an hour but saw nothing.

Alba was the first to turn and head back to the quarry. She knew there was something wrong as she spiraled down the cliff face on the air currents. Always the owlets maintained persistent pleas for food. Now there was silence. No, there was a sound. An owl cry, sure enough, but not of hunger. This was of fear, a spasmodic chittering hiss like the spitting of a frightened cat. As she swooped swiftly, anxiously towards the rubble of the shed, she glimpsed the long sinewy shape of a polecat vanishing among the rat runs. In its jaws had been a large drooping stubble-feathered bundle.

She flew down below the leaning timber and landed at the nest. Her mew of distress reached Tyto as he descended to join her.

The nest was silent. On the ledge, two dead and bleeding owlets bore mute testimony to the killing instinct of the polecat, slaying more than he needed to eat. In a dark crevice among the quarry debris, the third nestling was even now being torn apart and devoured. The cry of fear was issuing from the fourth chick, the only one able to fly, which had fluttered in a frenzied panic from the lithe, darting killer and had landed on the top of a post, propped against the rock face. He clung there, precarious but safe, calling desperately for his parents.

Tyto and Alba, distraught, landed near him and answered his cries with gentle, guttural grunts. Soon the young owl quieted. Only then did the two adult owls give vent to their grief, flying in aimless circles round and round the quarry, mewing shrilly as though in pain. In their circling, they swooped in turn above the ledge where the downy feathers of their dead young rippled in mock life on the stiffening bodies.

The mourning flight of the two owls continued unabated until the living claimed their attention. Var, the young owl, his fear evaporated, gave vent to cries of hunger, and this sudden resumption of normality sent Tyto to the quarry entrance where he fanned above the undergrowth, seeking the giveaway signs. It was a foretaste of things to come that it was ten minutes before Tyto stooped and rose with a squealing young rat. A month ago, a few seconds was all it would have taken.

Alba and Tyto resumed their place on the nesting ledge. With the indifference that considerate Nature allows its creatures to speedily adopt, they scuffed the torn carcasses of their young over the edge, to fall among the rotting timbers and the nettles. There, once again, the rats preyed on their predators. Var, afraid to attempt the upward flight back to the ledge to join his parents, sat clutching his perch, tight-clawed and unmoving. For the rest of that night and on into the next day, despite encouraging calls and beckoning flight forays by both adults, he sat there with the wind ruffling his plumage, almost toppling him. At midday a buzzard soared above the quarry and descended, and its shrill unfamiliar scream put the strength of fear to Var's wings and he lifted himself off with hurried wing-beats. When he reached the ledge where both Tyto and Alba were watching the approaching buzzard, he landed without mishap, and walked to a spot between the two where he sat, safe and puffed with pride.

The buzzard, the first to visit the quarry since the owls had arrived, continued circling, his eyes, as keen as owl eyes, seeing the telltale signs of rodents. Down, down he circled, huge within the confines of the walls, until he was gliding silently above the tangle of dead nettles and vetch and bracken and ragwort. Then his great wings folded upwards, pushing his body with its outflung claws down swiftly to a rat that had mistaken the gliding shadow for a harmless stock dove. The buzzard swung away and up and settled on the quarry wall. He tore into his prey with relish, his eyes already spotting the swaying of disturbed grasses far below. He was encouraged by this discovery of a new hunting ground. When he left, he would return with his mate. In the darkness of the tangled bramble thickets below, the polecat shared the same satisfaction over the same discovery. All around, the barren hills were already bleak with ominous winter winds, offering predators nothing to compare with the bounty that was here for the taking.

13

Survival

The chill November mists, which probed every gully and crevice in the windswept hills, gave way to unrelenting winds from the North that brought premature flurries of snow. The early warning signs were proving only too accurate, and by mid-December snow cloaked the slopes with uneven folds and the predators were driven further afield for their food. The rabbits on the lower heathlands were decimated by the buzzards and the long-eared owls, as well as by marauding weasels. The pair of peregrines gave up the high lonely reaches and visited the farm, where mice darted nervously around the sheep pens and the chickens left their coops only for the bran the farmer scattered. Above the sheep huddled in their pens an unfamiliar bird swept like a killer swallow, fork tail skimming the snow as he scattered the sheep dung in passing, picking at the beetles. When the farmer saw the rare red kite so near to his farm, he knew things were bad.

More and more hunters discovered the quarry. Two buzzards now roosted on the far wall, a hundred yards from the roost of the three owls. Every day Tyto would catch a glimpse of the two polecats which now quartered the undergrowth, while in the entrance of the quarry a family of five weasels had established itself, hunting as a pack with relentless planned ferocity which never left them hungry. All these were resident. Visiting predators reduced the rodent colony still further. The kite patrolled and took what carrion he could; a peregrine stayed for several days, catching several rats, but finding the confines of the quarry a handicap to his meteoric stoops, he flew off to try his skill among the redwings flocking to the hollies at the farm. Occasional kestrels hovered near the cliff face, snatching the meals they needed.

Amid all this predatorial competition, Tyto, Alba and Var continued to succeed each night in catching enough for their needs. But nightly, as the rat population declined, the task grew more difficult. Tyto made wider and wider forays over the surrounding countryside. These were seldom successful, even with Tyto's consummate hunting skills. The land was foreign to him, to his kind; only the quarry colony had kept him there in the first place. Now the land was covered with snow, and there was no prey there to be caught. The birds—linnets, fieldfares, redwings, lapwings, curlews, stonechats, the ubiquitous pipits —had all made for the lower woodlands, miles away, beyond the knowledge of Tyto and his family. In a barren land, landmarks hidden by the winter cloak, Tyto did not intend to fly outside the reach of the only safe roost he knew, and the only source of food he knew, however rapidly it was diminishing.

And rapidly diminishing it was. By the turn of the year, the ironic swing of Nature's pendulum was on the turn. Only a score of rats now remained, doomed by the tightening stranglehold of the natural food chain. An abnormality was about to be put to right. The superabundance of grain had now been eaten by the superabundance of rats it had fostered. There was no other food for them. The rank weeds and refuse were deep under snow, held fast in the impenetrable grip of rock-splitting frosts such as the hills had not known for half a century. The surviving rats were big, male rats who had managed to outwit their predators by sheer intelligence and cunning. But now they were starving. They fought among themselves, eating their own kind. The weasels killed the wounded survivors. Inevitably, the day dawned on the quarry when not one rat remained alive, nor any other rodent. Now it was the turning point for the predators.

The buzzards were the first to leave. Their slow, circling hunting flight took them further and further over the white-blanketed landscape to the distant woods and fields, where the snow lay thinner and wildlife thrived under cover. There came a day when they did not return. The polecats, male and female, after unsuccessfully trying to catch one of the weasels, slunk out of the quarry and followed the long frozen tracks of a vole that had fled in vain from the hurtling pursuit of the kite. Now the quarry was shared only by the owls and the weasels.

The night at the end of the gray, bitter mid-January

day was even colder; the northeast wind swayed the heavy, snow-laden, frozen twigs and branches of the quarry's elders and hawthorns in a slow mocking dance; the sky was almost clear, moonless but star-studded above the low, swiftly moving clouds. Tyto flew from the shelter of the well-protected roost and soared upwards to the top of the quarry face. He knew the quarry was bereft of prey, for his last rat had been caught three nights ago. For the past two nights, he had quartered the hill slopes in the direction of the distant farm. He had discovered that, at frequent intervals along the rough stone track from farm to quarry, hay and straw had fallen from the trailer behind the tractor. These sparse heaps, with their heads of rye grass, provided food for the voles that found them, and Tyto had caught two this way. He glided in the following wind, scouring the frozen path with Alba close behind.

Var, meanwhile, more through force of habit than anything, was quartering the quarry floor. His youthful inexperience would not easily accept the transition from plenty to nothing and a score of times he stalled, thinking the stiffened grasses were swayed by something other than the wind. Var was a big male for his age, having benefited from the rich surplus of food during his fledgling days. His hunting skill had developed quickly, though he had not yet once caught anything other than rats. His last meal had been two nights ago, when he had shared with a short-eared owl the remains of the hare Tyto had found on the hills. More and more of the predators were resorting to carrion when fresh kills were so rare.

Var's head bobbed as he fanned above the frozen weeds.

This time there was no mistake. The dark form of an animal was running swiftly, silently through the snow-capped tangle of undergrowth, disturbing nothing but nevertheless tracked by the owl's keen eyes and ears as accurately as though it were in the open. The weeds thinned and the dark shape scuttled silently across the frosted ground. A swoop and Var's talons plucked it into the air. A second later, Var knew that it was not a rat he had caught, for this creature fought with a ferocity no rat had ever shown. Instinctively, as the long sinewy shape almost wriggled from his grasp, Var swiveled a toe on one of his claws, strengthening the power of his grip. Higher and higher he flew, out through the quarry entrance on over the open ground, hovering with his fiercely struggling prey, trying in vain to stab it with his beak in mid-air.

Var had caught a full-grown female weasel, and even as her life was being crushed away, the animal fought with strength that put the outcome in the balance. Var swiveled the toe of the other claw, but with a fierce twist of her lithe body, the weasel clamped her jaws on Var's lower leg. The pain of this bite to the bone brought cries of distress from the young owl. Frantically he pecked at the head locked on his leg, and his bill struck deep into the weasel's skull. By now, they were fifty feet above the frozen hillside, and it was clear that Var was in danger. Tyto and Alba, though some distance away, picked up his cries and returned immediately. Tyto reached the distressed owl first but there was nothing he could do except circle, calling anxiously. Alba, behind him, echoed his frustration.

The weasel was mortally wounded by the blow to her head. In a last desperate attempt to avoid the stabbing bill, she loosened her jaws from Var's leg and transferred them in a flash to his throat, where they fixed with the implacability of death itself. Shaking his head as his life drained from him, Var twisted and turned, then flapped in a last frenzy. Owl and weasel plummeted to the ground, locked in an embrace in which both predators had become prey. Tyto and Alba wheeled slowly above, helpless and incomprehending. A halo of crimson formed around the mound of fur and feathers; then a gust of wind covered it lightly with powdered snow.

There was no let-up in the weather for the whole of January. Somehow Tyto and Alba managed to survive. Fortunately, the roost was ideal, the shelter formed by the fallen timber now made completely windproof by packed, frozen snow so that the cavity on the ledge provided perfect protection. But finding enough food to live on was a battle that they were slowly losing. Night after night, often in the face of stinging sleet and snow, the two owls would cover a circuit sometimes six miles in circumference. Their nocturnal hunting skills, though as sharp as ever, were of no avail in a land where there were hardly any creatures to be seen or heard. But once in a while they had success. On a night when the snow was easing off just before the dawn, Tyto caught a whisper in the wind and followed it to see a rabbit with an injured leg stumbling helplessly to escape from a rapidly approaching weasel. Neither animal heard or saw the owl until Tyto stooped and snatched the exhausted rabbit just as the weasel was within striking distance. Hissing in angry frustration, the weasel pawed the air as he watched the big white owl flying laboriously with his limp prey off up the hill, where another owl circled, calling in eagerness. An hour later nothing but the tiniest tufts of fur and a few large, broken bones remained in the snow, as two satisfied birds returned to their roost and a winter's day of side-by-side warmth.

Too many nights passed without success, and Tyto and Alba took to hunting in the day. This, too, brought little reward. Neither bird ever had enough to eat and Tyto, slightly the smaller of the two, began to find the long quartering flights an effort, with the result that his hunting range decreased instead of increased. Alba managed to fly further, and she caught the occasional field vole or pipit which kept them going. If the weather had not broken in the first week of March, both birds would have died of starvation. But the wind dropped and the snow began to melt and, though the winter was far from over, the water-filled gullies and the reappearance of the bracken from its armor of frozen snow did bring out enough foraging shrews and beetles to keep starvation at bay. With each passing day, Tyto and Alba gradually recovered their lost weight and strength.

At Holdern Farm, the snow had stayed packed and frozen for two months. Sam Holdern's crops sprouted later than he could ever remember, and his cows used up every last bale of his precious hay, which he had hoped not to exhaust. Then the melt came, and within a few days the fields were transformed from ice to rich swollen soil bursting to push forth the first of the crops. It was on the fourth evening after the thaw began that John Holdern saw something which revived the hopes he had cherished all winter long.

John had just helped his father herd in the cows from a day's grazing. Although the field was partly water-logged, the cows had gamboled like lambs at the sheer luxury of being able to stretch their limbs and eat fresh grass after two months of snow-enforced confinement in the barn. Herding the five reluctant cows back at dusk, for the night frosts were still severe, had proved difficult and tedious and John and his father were glad to swing the door shut. John followed his father across the yard, but suddenly stopped halfway, saying nothing, his attention caught by a gray shape on the pylon halfway across the five-acre.

John squinted in the half-light, his heart thumping. His father had reached the house and had stopped at the door, waiting.

"What's the matter, John. Seen something?"

"I'm not sure, Dad." John was not going to commit himself until he was certain.

His father grunted impatiently and went into the house. It was too cold to stand about. But he could guess what was keeping his son. Ever since the fire, the boy had thought every distant flying bird was a barn owl. It was almost an obsession. While he had to admit to himself that he missed the owls about the place—their hissing and snoring, the eerie screech breaking the twilight stillness, the silent white forms weaving among the ricks and out-buildings, where there was no doubt the number of mice had increased—even so, he could not understand John's unrelaxing watch for the bird. Admittedly, he had put up the owl nest-box that John had made, under the roof of the new barn, but he had told himself that his motives for doing so were more those of a practical farmer, keen to keep rodents under control, than those of a man with affection for the birds. He would welcome owls back, there was no denying it, but the chances were remote, for it seemed barn owls were becoming rarer all the time.

Outside, John stood motionless, peering at the distant pylon. The shape had not moved but it was familiar—excitingly, unbelievably familiar. Could this really be the first barn owl to visit the farm since the fire last July? John planned his route, then moved forward slowly and quietly to get behind the barn corner. From there, he tiptoed across to the hawthorn hedge and now he could look through, half concealed, though if it were an owl, he knew it would have seen his every move.

And it was an owl. An adult barn owl, too distant to tell whether male or female. Minutes after John had moved it lifted off, and the sight of the pale giant moth shape with its unearthly silent grace and dignity brought a lump to John's throat. He watched and willed it to come over to the house and discover the owl-box in the barn. It flew closer but glided down above the flooded field corner, fanning for a second, then dropping, and off again with a field mouse in its claws.

The bird flew back to the pylon. John could see its quick movements as it swallowed the prey. A short pause, a moment to preen an untidy breast feather which spiraled like a snowflake, and the bird was away. This time it flew with slow deliberation to the field corner and on, across the road, and behind the row of poplars out of sight. John stayed for ten more minutes, shivering in the cold, his eyes watering, then returned to the house. The owl was gone. Perhaps it had been one of the young hatched out at the farm, returning more by instinct than intent; or perhaps it was a total stranger passing through on the lookout for a mate. Either way, John Holdern was never to know, for the bird did not return.

14

The Intruders

The quarry had changed character almost totally. By the end of March the stark, frozen crater blasted out of the granite hills was like a garden, green with the plants and flowers which had burst forth in eager abundance once the restraint of frozen snow had gone. The nettles and scabious sent up new tall stems from the flattened debris of the old; wall pennywort raised bud-heavy heads above the clinging wild thyme, and the heather spread and thickened, ready to bloom. The wildlife flourished too, though in a different way now that the rats had gone. The overcrowded rodent population had resorted to young juicy roots for food and the plants had been kept down unnaturally. Now the quarry floor became a tangled jungle which, in turn, brought back the insects and insect-feeders; a pair of wrens began to build on the far wall; shrews found the tangled jungle of weeds across the quarry floor a haven for their foraging; for the first time since they had taken up residence in this alien new territory, the food available to Alba and Tyto was nearer to the natural diet they sought, though still far from ideal. With this return to near-normality, the two owls mated. In the second week of April, Alba laid her first egg. The day following, their presence in the quarry was discovered by hunters of the kind they had learned to fear most.

Two photographers, Peter Jackson and his wife Valerie, had been touring the area for a week, making a film for television on the wildlife of this range of central Welsh hills. They had decided on the creatures they were going to film when the man, on a squally, sunny early-April afternoon, glimpsed a bird that puzzled him. A closer look with binoculars gave him the unmistakable view of an adult male barn owl quartering the barren scrub-covered slope above the quarry. He lowered the glasses in amazement. It was not a species he had ever seen in these hills, and he knew them well; nor was it usual to see a barn owl so brazenly hunting by daylight. He hurried back to the camper where his wife was brewing tea.

Unaware that he was being observed, Tyto snatched a young rabbit from the bracken and returned to the quarry. He glided down to take the gift to Alba, who clucked affectionately as she heard the downward whisper of her mate's wings above the roost. Seconds later, she was tearing at the rabbit's carcass while Tyto proudly preened the feathers of her wings.

At dawn next day, Alba laid her second and final egg.

Though the food supply was improved, an instinctive regulating force came into play to guide her female pro-creativity. Two eggs were all that she should lay. Not this spring, in this territory, with this food supply, was a brood of five or six young owls to be reared.

Later that same morning, the quarry was visited for the first time in many months by humans. The glimpse of Tyto had convinced the enthusiastic husband and wife photographers that here was a subject much too out-of-the-ordinary to miss. It had not taken Peter Jackson long to locate the nest. There were not many hidden cavities where a pair of owls could hide, and after examining holes and crevices among the rocks and timber rubble he spotted the scattering of casts and regurgitated pellets below the propped-up beams. Clambering awkwardly up onto the rotting planks he heard the warning hiss from behind the fallen roof and he knew he had found the nest. To make sure, he persevered in his climb and peered through the cracks, to be greeted by an angry squawk from Tyto which almost, but not quite, caused him to lose his balance. Triumphant, the man returned to his equally excited wife.

For the next two hours Tyto stayed with Alba, tense and nervous, but refusing to leave her side, as the photographers, with more enthusiasm than sensitivity, set up a tripod and a camera with a zoom lens only ten feet from the opening to the nest. A small portable generator powering an infrared lamp for filming at night was rigged up nearby. Having thoroughly terrified the two owls, the couple retired to their van in the quarry entrance to wait till dusk.

The presence of the photographers and the van completely altered the natural cycle of the night. Tyto, who could hear every movement, did not venture out to hunt, though he knew Alba was hungry, as he was himself. The shrews foraged only within reach of their holes; a fox about to inspect the quarry gave it a wide berth when he heard the clatter of a kettle lid. Excited at the prospect and proud of their patience, the two film-makers, enjoying the distant sounds of the night, waited beside their equipment. After two hours and no move from Tyto or Alba, nor any other creature in the quarry, the man's patience began to ebb.

"I can't think why that male doesn't go hunting," he said, in a loud whisper to his wife.

"Perhaps he's not hungry," she whispered back.

"They both have to eat," replied the man, shortly.

They waited in silence for another hour. Neither owl made a sound.

"Are you sure they're there, Peter?" asked the woman.

"I'll check." The man stood up and began to walk gingerly along the rotting timber beam.

"Don't frighten them!" said his wife.

Her husband nodded. Then the timber broke under his weight and a piece fell with a crash and a shower of fibrous dust. Recovering his balance, he edged forward until he had reached the uprights which formed the shelter above the nesting ledge. A few feet away, Tyto puffed himself up aggressively as Alba trembled beside him, determined to defend her eggs to the last.

The man took out his torch and shone it between the cracks. The sudden light caused Tyto to wince and he bobbed his head in distress.

"They're still there," the man called. "I won't disturb them. I'll make the opening bigger so we can film them as they fly in and out."

So saying, the naturalist photographer tugged at the heavy timber and shifted it so that the ledge was more exposed. Having rectified this imperfection of the owl's choice of nest-site, the man returned to his wife at the camera.

That night Alba and Tyto went without food, remaining hunched and tense at their nest while the sound of their enemies persisted almost till dawn. Finally the two disappointed photographers packed up their equipment and returned to the van, where they had hot drinks and slept till midmorning.

At midday, Tyto left Alba and glided out into the quarry. The van had driven off, for Peter Jackson and his wife had found a pair of buzzards nesting in an old crow's nest in a spruce by the reservoir. By chopping off the obstructive surrounding branches, they were confident of filming as never before the natural home life of the buzzard.

Tyto caught a mole on the heathland a mile from the quarry. He immediately flew back with it to Alba, who took it from him, chittering with appreciation. Then Tyto flew off to see to his own needs, and snatched a young gray squirrel from the grove of hazels at the foot of the hill slopes. When he had devoured that, he flew down to the waterlogged ground at the foot of the bushes and bathed in the cold clear water contained in the grassy hollows. The bath refreshed and cleaned him, and he flew to the upper branches of a hazel, where he spent an hour preening himself contentedly. After gently hiccuping a pellet, he returned to the nest in early afternoon to roost for the rest of the day.

The photographers returned well before dusk. As before, they set up not only the camera, but the power as well. When darkness fell, the area of the nest was bathed in infrared light. The pattern of the previous night was repeated, with Tyto and Alba remaining defensive and frightened on their nest.

By midnight the patience of Peter Jackson was exhausted. His earlier filming of the buzzards had not gone as well as expected—the birds had circled all day without landing, leaving four eggs unprotected—and now he was faced with the problem of owls who never flew by night, going against all his preconceived knowledge. It was with exasperation, therefore, that he decided that if the birds would not come to him, so to speak, then he must go to the birds. So he dismantled the timber props that shielded the nest, totally exposing Alba, who crouched puffed and frightened on her two precious eggs. Tyto, twice his normal size, bobbed and weaved and hissed aggressively as the camera motor turned in the unnatural glow that worried his eyes. Bewildered and angry, Tyto took to flight, making stooping mock-attacks at the two humans and the huge reflecting eye that followed his every move.

Now the eye concentrated on Alba. She tolerated its relentless stare as long as she could, but finally her fear became greater than her protective instinct and for the first time for ten days, Alba flew from the nest. Immediately, the temperature level of the eggs, vital to successful incubation, began to fall.

For two hours the photographers waited for the owls

to return, desperately keen to capture on film that grace-
ful, silent, stretched descent and landing at the nest of the
parent birds, but the wait was in vain. The two owls could
be glimpsed circling, dark against the stars, pale against the
quarry wall, but, frustratingly, they did not land. The
camera team gave up at dawn and dismantled their equipment.

An hour later, after no movement from the van, where
the couple was asleep, the owls returned. Peter Jackson
had made an attempt to replace the timber over the ledge,
but he had left gaps and the protection was not as good as
it had been previously. Rain would now fall directly onto
the nest, though fortunately, the day promised to be fine.

It took Alba a long while to return to the nest. The eggs
were faintly warm and her body quickly restored them
to the right temperature, though inside one of them the
temperature drop had slowed the metabolic rate of growth
of the embryo chick to a point from which it would never
recover.

That day Tyto killed and brought to Alba a mouse and
two young curlews, which he had caught without diffi-
culty while quartering the hill in the afternoon sun. As
the day was drawing to a close, both owls on the ledge
heard the familiar sound of the van returning.

Peter Jackson and his wife had, by a combination of
luck and patience, succeeded in getting their best-ever
shots of a polecat's nest. They had inevitably disturbed it,
in a hole in the giant trunk of a fallen beech, and the
female had transferred the three young to a safer hole
below ground. It was this transferring that the camera had
captured in every detail. In fact, they had shot so much

footage that they were now considering, if the birds such as the owls and buzzards continued to be so uncooperative, that they could put together a half-hour film on the life of the polecat. But one more attempt to film the owls was going to be made.

Through the timber propped above the ledge, Tyto and Alba watched the approach of the van. They saw the two dreaded figures making their way towards them. As on the previous nights, they heard and saw the camera and the light set up a few yards from them. Again Tyto stayed. He could feel Alba trembling beside him and his own fear was apparent in the way he huffed out his feathers and adopted an aggressive posture. This relentless interference night after night into their nesting routine was more disturbing than any natural interruption. An attack, whether by another bird, animal or even human, was more understandable than this furtive pressure.

The timber was gently moved so that the two owls were in clear focus. The motor, silent to the photographers but audible to both owls, purred like a distant cat, gloating, waiting. The owls, tensed and nervous, waited as they had waited for three nights, for the attack that never came.

There was a thud on the ledge beside them. It was a dead field vole. Peter Jackson had had the inspired notion of trapping several during the day, hoping to use them to coax the owls into interesting behavior.

He was disappointed. Tyto's head bobbed as he eyed the human-scented untouchable carcass, while Alba, her eyes watchful for frontal attack, ignored it completely. Another thud as a second vole hit the rock and fell to the ground. Still the owls did not move.

An hour passed and Alba, her fear increasing as the motionless eye held her fixed in its sight, trembled more violently. Her beak gaped, a sure sign of distress.

"I believe the female's hungry," said the photographer to his wife in a whisper that sent the shrews in the quarry squeaking for cover.

Peter Jackson tossed his third and last dead vole. Now, perhaps, he would actually film an owl swallowing a vole in one gulp. The vole, badly aimed, struck Alba on the breast. She squawked in terror and flew in a panic from the ledge, her wildly beating wings buffeting Tyto. Her legs struck one of the eggs, which rolled to the edge of the ledge, where it spun slowly to a standstill, half on and half off, poised above a sheer drop.

The camera lens zoomed in to capture the drama, then pulled back and tracked with Tyto as he took off after his mate, following her into the darkness to disappear out of range and focus.

Tyto flew swiftly, spurred on by Alba's cries of distress. When he caught up with her, he mewed softly and she answered. Both knew what must now happen, but for a moment they lingered, wheeling silently high above the quarry and their violated nest, bidding it farewell. And then suddenly the owls were away over the hillside, without a backward glance, heading for the distant farm and the fields beyond.

15

The Return

Tyto and Alba flew five miles that night, stopping only twice to rest and drink. It was as if they had agreed to put as much distance as possible as quickly as possible between themselves and the scene of eight months of drama and hardship. The buoyancy of their flight seemed to reflect their relief as they left the hostile starkness of the land they had managed to outwit and began to fly over territory more akin to their nature. Bare slopes and crags gave way to fields and farms and villages. The glint of streams stirred in Tyto memories of greater expanses of water, and when, as the sky began to let in the approaching day, he glimpsed the sheen of pools across a stretch of marshland, he knew this was where they would stop, at least for the present.

Wing-weary, stirred by feelings beyond their understanding, the two owls glided down to the familiar, welcome scent and whispering movement of a willow tree. There, unworried, except by the need for food, they settled and rested, more at ease with their surroundings, with life itself, than they had been for many a month.

Dawn was unfurling its softer light from the still pools among the rushes and willow herb when Tyto lifted himself gently from the tree. Gliding above the tall reed mace, he drank in the familiar sounds and scents and sights, and when he saw the blunt-nosed arrow of a vole paddling unhurriedly across the stream, Tyto fanned above it for several seconds, almost as though he preferred to watch it than kill it. Then he dropped and plucked the vole from the water without causing a ripple. A stab in mid-flight stilled the creature's silent struggle and Tyto flew back to the willow. He passed Alba, who was hovering above one of the shallow pools which was almost solid with the glutinous globules of frog-spawn. A guttural chorus of frogs advertised their presence, and Tyto saw Alba descend slowly and grab one in her claws. Seconds later she joined Tyto back in the tree, where they devoured their meal.

That day the two owls ate between them three voles, two moorhen chicks, a reed bunting and several more frogs. In the shady canopy of the willow, they roosted from midafternoon until the marshy pools began to darken with the shadows of approaching night.

Tyto was the first to move. He flew from the willow

to soar above the swaying reeds and golden marsh mari-
golds, reveling in the hunting ground that stretched, lush
and fresh and richly stocked, for a mile to the surrounding
slopes. Apart from the house adjoining a garage on the
road that cut through the marshland there were no human
habitations, and the area was as perfect a hunting ground
as any owl could want. Tyto's pleasure and satisfaction at
this welcome reversal of his situation showed in the way
he soared and swooped and skimmed the rush-tips, letting
them brush his breast and underwing, and then down,
scattering the midge-dances above the water crowfoot and
the lilies. At a neighboring pool Alba fanned above the
scuttling shape of a vole through the reeds. Tyto flew
across to her as she snatched the struggling prey and encouraged her with soft cries as she headed for the willow.
Tyto could sense that Alba, like himself, would be happy
to make this territory their own. But that was not to be.

The first inkling Tyto had that things were too good to
be true was when he caught the last vibrations of a scream
from half a mile across the swaying sedge, a scream that
told him that another of his kind was hunting the same
area, and staking a claim.

Tyto drifted to the willow and settled on the topmost
slender twigs, which bent under his weight. He clung
there, head bobbing, as he surveyed the horizon. The
miniscule white dot would have escaped the eyes of any
creature but himself. But Tyto saw it clearly enough, and
his feathers fluffed in instinctive anticipation of the confrontation he knew was to come.

From an alder tree fifty yards away, Alba called softly.
She, too, had seen the white shape approaching, joined

now by a second. Tyto replied with a nervous grunt and then took off from his precarious perch. He flew towards the oncoming owls, knowing he and Alba had been spotted long ago. Already, Tyto was adopting the attitude of the aggressor. He—and Alba—were the attackers, the upstart invaders who had arrived to dispute the sovereignty of a territory already claimed by two of their own kind. The natural laws of such a conflict tended to give the edge to the defenders, who instinctively fought harder to preserve what they had won than attackers who were trying to take a new territory. So when the two adult males flew towards each other, puffed and chittering, the greatest anger was in the heart of the defender, and their first buffeting collision told Tyto that he was up against the most determined adversary he had yet met.

The male owl that Tyto was challenging was a four-year-old and the victor of three years of battles such as this. Though no bigger than Tyto, he fought with more experience and more cunning. Unlike Tyto, he had wintered well and his strength had not been sapped by near starvation. Again and again the two flew at each other, throwing out talons at the last split second, clawing a burst of downy feathers from the breast or flanks of the other. Alba circled distantly, screaming with anxiety, while the mate of the defending owl, a yearling female, flew in so close that Tyto thought she too was about to attack him.

The female owl was Ula, Tyto and Alba's own offspring.

After Ula had been chased from her parents' territory in the autumn she had made her way to the marsh, where she had wintered alone for three months. Then, when the ice began to melt, she had met the male and, although they had not yet mated, it had been clear from the start that they would pair up. Although only a few months had passed since Ula and Tyto and Alba had flown, hunted and roosted together, the natural need for recognition had disappeared, and the three did not recognize each other now. Even if they had, Ula's mate would not have relaxed his fierce defense of the territory he claimed, and Tyto would not have ceased his challenge to take the territory for his own. To Ula, the two adult owls were challengers to the rights of her mate and herself. To Tyto, as to Alba, Ula was an alien stranger. Yet as the younger bird's persistent mewing reached his ears, a faint memory rippled through Tyto of a similar hunger-pleading call, but it quickly passed.

The battle drew to its foregone conclusion: the triumph of the greater wiles and experience of the older bird. Tyto flew defeated from the marsh, chased by the victory-chittering owl. Alba and Ula, mother and chick, followed their respective mates without a sign of recognition in passing.

The defeat left Tyto ruffled and upset. His left flank was bleeding from a talon scratch and his neck had several deep nicks from his adversary's bill. As soon as Tyto knew he was out of sight of the victorious owl which had returned with Ula to the marsh, he flew wearily to the roof of a signal box at the side of a railway track. Alba settled beside him, and her solicitous grunts and gentle preening of his ruffled wing feathers calmed and comforted him.

The two owls stayed on the roof until dawn. It was only the arrival of the signalman, with his shoulder bag of breakfast flask and sandwiches, that disturbed them. The man stopped and stared up, startled, when the two white shapes lifted from the roof and flew to the cover of the ash trees further down the track. Now he saw what they were, he watched them with no great surprise, taking them for the two white owls he had seen several times before from the road across the marsh.

That night, for no reason other than the cycle of the moon and the beckoning of the stars and the rising of the sap and the sighing of the wind, Tyto courted Alba as he had done an age ago, with flank-to-flank, head-bobbing, neck-turning, bill-clacking, soft, chattering affection. The spirit of spring was in their mating and in the chasing flight of ecstasy that followed across the railway and the road and the outskirts of the marsh to the swaying poplars, where they finally came to rest among the moon-silvered whispering leaves.

They did not begin to hunt for food till dawn, and then they flew from their resting place in the poplars towards the distant glinting water they had been staring at for hours. When they reached the river, for the river it was, Tyto was too filled with restlessness to hunt. Alba quartered the banks and caught a vole as it ran from its grazing in the field. Tyto flew up and down the river, calling excitedly, not knowing what was troubling him, only that he was troubled. Alba, when she had eaten her catch, flew alongside him, infected by his unease. Eventually, as an early shower ended and the sun came through, the two owls headed for the giant oak that stood a few yards from the riverbank. There, in the oak's green darkness, Tyto nervously preened his damp plumage, while Alba churred worriedly beside him.

The day passed peacefully. By evening Tyto was calmer and, with Alba, he glided from the tree sharp and eager for the hunt. The very air above the river seemed to impart a greater vigor to him. Skimming low above the rippling river which had been a natural part of his existence since his first days of flight, Tyto felt with all his being that to continue to survive, he must be within the river's call. He heard the calling now, an echo from fifty miles away, urging him to leave the hostile and the untried and come back to the familiar and the proven.

As the darkness grew and the moon rose full and the sky filled with blazing stars, the two owls hunted and ate their fill. Below the oak, the owls' casts and pellets were discovered by a foraging hedgehog. Alba flew to the willow, where she devoured a water vole. Tyto took a flapping dabchick to the bank and killed and ate it, leaving a debris of feathers and legs, then flew up to the willow. But he did not settle. He circled the tree, calling, urging, and Alba understood. There was a nest site to be found and eggs to be laid. Without a sound she drifted after him, as Tyto ceased his circling and his calling and flew on a purposeful course towards the beckoning stars in the East, following the winding moonlit thread that led the way.

The journey took four nights and days, less time than the westward flight the previous summer. Both birds had become accustomed to flying in daylight and they covered several miles between dawn and dusk. People at pleasure or at work along the river remarked upon the rare sight of two adult barn owls pursuing a course more frequently taken by long-necked swans. Occasionally Tyto departed from the river and crossed the countryside, never once losing his sense of direction. In this way the journey passed without incident, and, after a long rest roosting in an ivy-clad elm for most of the third day, they set out at dusk. Within an hour they came in sight of the water tower.

Tyto circled the familiar spot, and his screech stilled the rustling waterfowl and grazing voles. Then he flew to the tower, where he flapped frustratedly against the wire mesh which still barred his way to the sheltered nesting site behind.

The water tower, familiar though it was, was not his destination. Circling in a wide sweep beyond the tower, he flew again over the river and headed upstream, knowing Alba was behind him.

Tyto knew where he was going. It was over two years since his precipitate flight from Merford to the first territory he had made his own, yet now his instinct and inbuilt navigational skill was bringing him back without error or hesitation. And because it was precisely that original outward route retraced, it led him to the tower of Merford church.

Tyto flew towards the familiar shape, silvered on its moon side. He landed on the ledge below the window, but there was no longer any entrance here. The church, like the water tower, had been wired up with netting so that no pigeon, starling, sparrow or even a bat could find a way in and despoil the building. And certainly there was no opening left for an owl, not after the now-legendary visitation by a veritable demon-owl a while back. Tyto, frustrated, flew back to meet Alba and they settled side by side to rest on the church roof. Alba's bill was open and she was hunched with fatigue. The urgent aim of both birds now was to find a nesting site so that Alba could settle and lay eggs.

They stayed until dawn began to thin the edge of night and then took off. Again Tyto knew exactly where to go. Above the village green and the pond with the already waking ducks, over the roof of the Harrow Pub and the houses and the narrow road, across the fields past the pylon to the red-roofed farm and the giant red-roofed barn. Only now there was no barn; just a burnt-black patch of earth and the remnants of a wall. Frustrated yet again, Tyto wheeled above the farm. There were other barns, but these were modern, smooth and uninviting. Then he saw the hole, just below the apex of the roof of one of the shiny new buildings. Inside, just beneath the hole, was the nest box, put there by the willing father at his son's instigation. A large open tray some three feet long, divided by a low partition, it had been there since the barn had been erected in the autumn.

Tyto landed at the hole and hopped down inside. The section of the tray farthest from the entrance was perfect. He screeched a cry of triumph. The cry stretched out and pushed tentatively into the dreams of the boy asleep in the nearby farmhouse, but the boy merely frowned and did not wake. Alba answered the call and joined Tyto in the box, landing heavily, almost totally exhausted. Safe, secure, the two owls slept side by side for the rest of the day, recovering their strength.

That evening, John Holdern was returning from a darts match in the Harrow Pub, walking along the road, when he heard a sound that stopped him in his tracks. It was the insistent snoring of an owl, a familiar sound he had heard at the farm many times before, though not for many many months. He stopped and listened. There it was again, from the other side of the hedge, in the five-acre field adjoining

the farm. He hurried to the gate and stared across. In the
gathering dusk it was difficult to see, but the constantly
repeated sound seemed to be coming from the trees in the
far hedge.

John leaned on the gate and waited. His experience was
that the churring call was usually made when there was a
mate nearby. He tried to stop himself wondering about
the owl box his father had put up. The thought of owls
nesting in that would be too good to be true, so he decided
not to tempt providence by thinking of it. In any case, if
there was a pair, they would surely not have had time yet
to find the box, for he could swear no barn owls had been
back again before this moment.

He frowned. Funny, though, he had a vague recollection of dreaming of a barn owl only last night. His
thoughts were interrupted by the very sound he was trying to recall, the nerve-tingling screech that was like no
other cry in the world. He waited expectantly, looking in
all directions.

Then he saw it, a sight that never failed to thrill him in-
tensely—the unmistakable white shape of an adult barn
owl, gliding with uncanny silence and precision across the
stars towards the pylon. The bird hovered at the pylon,
then seemed to change its mind and flew towards the gate.

The owl spotted the boy and veered away. As the bird
turned, caught for a second in the full light of the moon,
the whiteness became a silver-gold that looked ethereal.
And the clarity of the vision revealed something else,
something that brought a look of disbelief to the face of
the spectator. The left wing of the bright, white owl had a
gap in the pinion feathers.

John Holdern stared, incredulous, unable to take in the

evidence of his own eyes. It had been more than two years since he had stood in the church porch and watched the disheveled white shape of the immature owl disappear into the distance; its left wing injured, feathers from it left lying on the floor of the nave. Apart from one or two glimpses of the bird in the weeks after that event, he had not seen it since. Yet as he watched this owl now winging across the field, he knew with unshakable certainty that it was the very same bird. The significance of the realization dawned on him like some kind of miracle.

"It's Whitey," he breathed, his eyes straining through the gloom. "It's Whitey, come back to where he was born."

Tyto drew near to the farm. In the box in the barn roof, Alba was about to lay her second clutch of the season. Tyto landed on the roof. Mice scuttled in the straw below, exactly as they had scuttled in another barn an age ago. In a moment he would glide down and catch one. Just now he was content to sit and gaze about him—at the farmhouse, with its curling wisp of smoke, at the distant river and the boathouse where early memories stirred, at the figure of the boy walking slowly down the road, his eyes returning Tyto's stare.

The boy saw the owl rise, glide and fan above the straw, then down, with claws outstretched and up again, clutching a struggling mouse. He watched the bird fly to the nest box and heard the cry of Alba as she took the gift, and his heart was filled to overflowing. Many times in the past months, John Holdern's thoughts had dwelled on the pressures that barn owls had to face from Nature and from humankind, and often he had wondered what fate had overtaken the owl he had called Whitey. Tonight, he could only marvel at their powers of endurance. He stood motionless in the road and waited.

Tyto flew from the nest across the field. As he flew, he shared the night wind's secrets. Then he turned and, with silent feathers glowing in the moon, he headed for the stars that lit the way to the survival of his kind.

AUTHOR'S NOTE: Between 1930 and 1967 the barn owl population in Great Britain fell from about 25,000 to 12,000, a decline of more than fifty per cent. Declared an endangered species, barn owls and their eggs were placed under special legal protection, and their numbers have made a small comeback. There are an estimated 15,000 barn owls in Great Britain today. But the barn owl's battle for survival as a species is far from over.